Amazing Dog Stories

David Wilk

Contents

Dedication

For my beloved Terryle. I will love you forever.

This book is dedicated to my wonderful canine friends who have brightened my life with their loving light:

Jenny

George Burns

Gracie Allen

Yosemite

George Burns II

Tinker

Petey

Acknowledgments

I would like to express my gratitude to the following individuals for reading rough drafts of this book while it was progressing and offering their guidance on how it might be improved:

Tamara Davis, Christine Palaia, Robin Mizrahi, Glenn Wilk, Ken Wilk, Susan Hartzler and Hildee Brahm.

Also, I want to thank the esteemed individuals whose quotes I used to introduce each chapter. These are among the finest dog appreciation quotes ever written:

Will Rogers, Caroline Knapp, Charles Schultz, Charles De Gaulle, Roger Karas, Mark Twain, Gene Hill, Laura Jaworski and Josh Billings.

A big thanks to Edna Clyne-Reky for the beautiful poem "Rainbow Bridge," which many of us know for its lovely projection of what happens when we're reunited with our beloved dogs in heaven.

Virtually all the photos were taken by Terryle Wilk and me, but one lovely photo of our puppies standing while nursing from Gracie was taken by my friend Janet Thompson.

Thanks additionally to my team at Amazon Publishing Assistant for assisting me in conducting a comprehensive marketing campaign on behalf of Amazing Dog Stories.

About the Author

David Wilk is an author and a lifelong dog lover. He has written two novels – Big City Fish and Gridlock – three non-fiction books and assisted on a screenplay for Gridlock. Sixteen years ago he was asked to write a biography for a private individual. He loved the project and has now written or ghost written 18 biographical books.

Prior to writing full time, Wilk was an entrepreneur who founded Professional Beach Volleyball and the Pro Beach Volleyball Tour, was co-founder and president of the online surf report and forecast Surfline and founded Pacific Milk Caps, a national distributorship during the Pogs boom of the mid-1990s.

Wilk currently resides in Oxnard Shores, California, with his wife Terryle (nickname "Tunes") and two dogs – Petey and Tinker.

If there are no dogs in heaven,
then, when I die,
I want to go where they went.

-Will Rogers

Introduction

Jenny – 1982

The first dog who ever captured my heart was a one-year-old Golden Retriever named Jenny. My girlfriend Terryle inherited Jenny from a surfer who was leaving on a year-long surf trip, and we were both immediately smitten by the sweetness and joyfulness of this young dog's personality. It didn't hurt that Jenny was gorgeous – with a fluffy coat, golden red fur, beautiful eyes and an expression that was equal parts earnest and friendly.

Jenny was full of affection for Terryle (whom I soon married), her young sons Travis and Tyler, and, fortunately, me. She savored being petted and would happily lavish sweet kisses in return. Jenny loved to play and would spend hours outside with the boys, but what she really loved was the beach. I guess being a surfer's puppy will do that. Jenny's particular hobby was chasing seagulls up and down the shoreline. She was a vision with her long legs galloping in sweet precision and her red-blonde hair pinned back by the swiftness of her stride as she ran almost to the horizon, then sprinted right back to us and right past.

She never caught a seagull, but for Jenny, the enjoyment was in the chase.

One thing I soon grew to admire was Jenny's loyalty. She would do anything for her human family and would tag along enthusiastically wherever we wanted to go. Travis and Tyler adored her. It was clear that our family was the most important thing in Jenny's life. Golden Retrievers want to be friends with anyone and everyone by their nature, but we always knew we were number one.

Jenny was 100 percent trustworthy. There was no deceit or dishonesty in her actions. What you saw was what you got. When Jenny was particularly happy or excited, her tail would wag furiously as she raced around the room because she just could not contain her pure joy. Jenny's enthusiasm was impossible to resist, and it instantly elevated everyone's mood.

I've read that a dog shows its affection by looking into your eyes, but I learned this firsthand with Jenny. She couldn't give me a hug but would give the most loving gazes while I touched or petted her. She was totally non-judgmental; I could look terrible, I could be in a bad mood, I could have had a discouraging business issue plague me all day, but Jenny's eyes always reflected unadulterated love.

Every morning just after sunrise, Jenny would wag her tail with excitement, and I would take her for a morning walk. She was so happy to be on this daily journey, and her ebullient mood transferred right to me. I still picture Jenny and me walking briskly in the cool morning air, up the hill above our house, with the coast down behind us, then back down to a panorama of the blue Pacific! It was a wonderful way to start our day.

When Terryle and I drove off for work in the morning, Jenny would lie down on the front porch to wait for our return. Whoever came home first was greeted by an excited red dog awakened from a snooze in the adjacent bushes, rushing out, tail wagging ferociously, grateful for the loving pets and eager to bestow loads of kisses in return.

As the years sped by, Jenny slowed down and could not do some of the things she loved. She still savored a trip to the beach, but now she just ambled after the seagulls overhead. She walked slower in the mornings. After a while, it became evident that she was in pain, and our veterinarian's test revealed the terrible diagnosis. It was cancer.

We all knew what had to come next, but none of us could bear it. Still, it was our responsibility out of the love for a cherished friend not to let her suffer. That last trip to the vet was profound heartbreak. No one else had the emotional resilience to come with me, I guess, so I went alone by default. I walked into the veterinarian's office, head held down, tears streaming. Jenny was braver than me. If you have had a beloved pet, you know the feeling. It is a sadness so deep that it can barely be endured.

Jenny brought our family so much joy during her twelve years with us that there was no doubt we should always share our lives with a dog...and we always did. Each and every one of our beloved pooches enriched and amazed us with its unique personality, its endearing character, its adventures and misadventures. Some were laugh-out-loud funny, a few were terrifying, and many were inspiring. Even though the experience of owning and loving your pet with all your heart inevitably ends in sadness, the joy that comes along the way makes it well worthwhile.

In thinking about each of our dogs, I realized that I had quite a few really good stories to tell. No doubt everybody does.

So here are a few of our dogs' most amazing stories as they intertwine with our own life stories.

(Note: These are individual stories and wind through the narrative of my own life. They are all true. I decided not to put the stories in the first half of the book in perfect chronological order because I wanted to mix them up a bit to make the pace of the book more interesting. The names of the dogs in the stories and the dates they took place are in bold at the beginning of each one. The second half does follow a chronological narrative.)

- **David Wilk**

Our first dog, Jenny, loved holidays and Cinco de Mayo was a particular favorite.

Chapter One: Swept Away

Before you get a dog, you can't quite imagine
what living with one might be like.
Afterward, you can't imagine living any other
way.

-Caroline Knapp

Gracie, Yosemite and George II – 2005

Terryle and I glanced down at the little stream that runs along the street below our house, looked at each other and shook our heads in wonder. It was no longer a little stream. Today, it was an absolute monster. We'd never seen it raging like this before. It was actually scary.

One of the unique aspects of living in our new house in the lovely Ojai Valley was that a stream flowed right alongside our street. Having a river or a stream so close is exceptionally rare for Southern California. There are millions of houses but not much flowing water.

7

Our three Golden Retrievers loved to swim in our little stream, and every time we walked them down from our hill to the street, they jumped in for a dip. In the summer and fall, the water flow was reduced to a trickle, but our dogs knew every deep spot that created a pool. Strolling along the lovely, tree-lined road to the dead end of our block, the dogs would hustle into the water three or four different times, then race up to rejoin us, dripping wet, ready to do it again.

In the other direction, down half a mile, the creek took a turn toward the ocean and actually crossed our road right before it emptied onto a two-lane highway. That meant that all of us residents had to drive across the stream any time we wanted to go to town or return home. Until the more recent years of severe drought, there was at least a small flow in our stream all year-round. It was fun splashing through the water in the car and lovely seeing the birds and occasional wildlife along the creek shore.

I liked to look for a pair of birds – an elegantly lanky, long-legged blue heron and a stocky, smaller, scruffy green heron – who were there fishing side-by-side almost every day right where the stream crossed our road, and cars drove through. Rain or shine, I could see them there, like it was their job.

Terryle nicknamed them Sammy and Moe just because they had become so familiar that they couldn't remain anonymous. The birds were absolutely non-plussed by the occasional passing car. They ignored any and all distractions and just continued looking down into the stream for food. Every once in a while, I would spot one or the other leaning in to snag a fish. That never failed to give me a laugh.

The portion of the stream we needed to cross each day was roughly twenty feet wide. There was a high-water crossing (a place where the road is elevated to facilitate crossing a stream) that we would drive over. Depending on the time of year, there were a few inches to perhaps a foot of water on top of the high water crossing for cars to splash through. It was different than any other streets we knew. Splashing through made it fun.

Neighbors cautioned us, though, that the water could reach a very high flow during a significant rainstorm, and it would be dangerous to cross. The uncharacteristically high water might persist for days, even after the rain stopped, due to flow down off the surrounding mountains. For the duration of the event, all of us neighbors would be stuck on the block and couldn't leave.

Sure enough, there were a few rainstorms our first few years that swelled the creek to a precarious level. Sustained rain would raise the water up and speed the flow to where only the bravest soul would venture across. That was not Terryle or me. (Neighbors who drove a truck had an advantage, but even they couldn't get across if the water was too high.)

So, on those occasions of significant rain, we contented ourselves with looking down at the roaring stream from the edge of our hill.

But this was different.

The rain we'd seen in this storm was epic. The deluge lasted for several days and the water level in the stream kept steadily rising. We could hear the roar from our house and see from our hill that the creek was now drastically overflowing its ten to fifteen-foot banks. It flowed hard for another 100 feet wide on the far side of its normal bed and came all the way across our road to our hillside on the close side. It was probably 150 feet wide in total, decimating everything in its path. Where it normally flowed at five or-so miles per hour, it was now churning with white water, loud and out of control, raging at many times its normal speed.

We were watching giant tree branches and whole trees being carried downstream. It was wild! We spotted a refrigerator, a barbecue, wood from construction, a nearly intact garden shed and all sorts of other debris being swept downstream. Neighbors below us on the street alongside the creek lost all their front yard gardens and decorations. One lost a lovely greenhouse. They were just overwhelmed and swept away. Another unfortunate couple had the elevated stream run right through the bottom floor of their house, and when they inspected the next morning, all the furniture was gone, replaced by mud.

Miraculously, no one was hurt.

This storm was not fun by any definition, and for days, no one on our street could get out. Even when the rain stopped, the flow continued, coming down from the mountains and raging away. We and our assorted neighbors would trudge through the mud to marvel at how powerfully the stream was roaring over our high-water crossing.

11

"I wouldn't want to cross THAT," someone would always say.

"Guess we won't be getting out today," another would add. "Your car wouldn't make it ten feet before being swept out of sight."

On one of these days, Terryle and I walked down to see the spectacle and took our three dogs with us. They had no reservations about plowing through mud, deep puddles or hopping over rocks and debris. Truth is, they liked that the best.

At this time, we had Gracie Allen (the mother of our one and only litter), who was eight years old, and two of her puppies, Yosemite and George Burns II, who were not quite five. We didn't have them on leashes, since there would be no cars to worry about on the road this day. They would never attack a neighbor, although running up to greet them, covered in mud, was way less welcomed than usual.

Gracie Allen (dog edition) was a unique and impressive character. She loved chasing the ball, seemed utterly fearless and was a great swimmer in freshwater or ocean waves. She had wowed us as a young puppy, swimming across a shallow river we were crossing while we were hiking with friends. It was an accident that she even got the chance. She was only four months old and had never been swimming before. A few people had started to wade through the knee-high water while we were still gathering some gear, and Gracie just walked in and swam right along with them. By the time we noticed her in the water, she was almost all the way across.

Gracie was smallish for a Golden Retriever, weighing in at around 65 pounds. She was on the blonde side of strawberry blonde, with redder sections and platinum blonde streaks down her rump. Her tail was amazingly bushy. We'd had her since she was a puppy, and she gave birth to a magical litter at age three-and-a-half. So, Gracie had a special place in our unofficial "Dog Hall of Fame" just for that. But she was a very adventurous dog, and several of the stories in this book are going to involve her.

Gracie was moderately obedient, but if she didn't want to do something Terryle or I wanted her to do, she would simply ignore us. She didn't make a big deal about it; she just chose to do her own thing instead of our own thing. She was sweet and loving but could be stubbornly independent. It was like she appreciated our advice but chose to do something else.

George Burns II and Yosemite were two of Gracie's puppies. George, like his mother, had a lot of blonde in his golden red coat with occasional white patches, a big head and was very handsome. He was tall and weighed 95 pounds, the heaviest of any of our line of Goldies, but he was not really overweight. Just long, tall and large.

George was a loyal and loving boy. He loved to be petted and would linger for an hour if you didn't stop. All in all, George was not particularly smart. He didn't really formulate his own ideas, instead tending to follow his sister Yosemite's lead on most matters. The only time he was in any way the alpha male was when we went walking. Then, he would take the lead and growl at the ladies if they tried to venture ahead of him. That probably annoyed Gracie and Yosemite, but they did comply.

Yosemite, or "Yoyo," as we called her, was incredibly smart and really in tune with humans. She was very red in color, with just a few white-blonde sections in her chest and back flank, and she weighed around 75 pounds. Yosemite knew what you were going to do before you even did it.

Going somewhere in the car? Yosemite would be outside next to the vehicle, waiting for you to walk out the door. Straightening up the house for guests? Yosemite would be on the driveway, looking for their arrival.

She followed instructions without us needing to repeat them. This was partly because she was obedient but also because Yosemite somehow knew what was coming and wanted to please us. When Terryle suffered from serious health problems, Yosemite stayed right with her, trying to provide as much comfort as she could. We marveled at Yosemite's sweetness.

Speaking of blondes, so you can picture her, Terryle is a beautiful blue-eyed blonde with mid-shoulder length, slightly curly hair and a smile that positively lights up the room. She is medium height with a slim physique, and she always dresses nicely. Her sense of style earns compliments wherever she goes.

Terryle is smart and funny, and a particular focus of her humor is making fun of me, which, I assure you, is not justified.

As for me, I am 5'8" with dark brown curly hair, brown, twinkly eyes, a moustache over a friendly smile (so I'm told) and a prominent nose. I dress somewhat respectably, mostly wearing jeans, and it is safe to say that Terryle outdresses me 365 days each year. Any style I have is thanks to her.

Walking down our block toward the stream crossing on that fateful day, Terryle and I joined up with some neighbors who were heading there, too. We compared stories of crazy things we'd see around our respective homes during this storm. One neighbor saw a van being swept out of sight. The stream was easily over 100 feet wide at the high-water crossing, flowing with a steady roar at thirty to forty miles per hour, with big, loud waves, bouncing, swirling water and all kinds of debris racing past. It looked more like a river than a creek. We all shook our heads in awe at the power of the swollen stream.

Suddenly, on the far side of the stream, our blue heron "mascot," Sammy, fluttered to the ground on the shallow edge of the flow. Before we knew it, Gracie leaped in to chase the tall bird and was immediately swept downstream and out of sight. We all looked on in horror and disbelief for a moment before gasping and screaming. Gracie, despite being a great swimmer, was not coming back. She had no control over the powerful flow. She was rising and falling with the violent, swirling waves, being tossed and spun every which way like all the other debris, completely disappearing for long moments, then bobbing to the surface again. Gracie was swept out of sight in seconds.

Just as we were gasping as we lost sight of Gracie, Yosemite leaped in, too. Like Gracie, she was instantly swept up in the turbulence, violently tossed around, spinning in circles, now underwater, now popping back up, swimming desperately, a diminishing form, gone in seconds as the river carried her away. Terryle grabbed George to make sure he didn't join in this nightmare situation. She was shrieking and crying, as were our neighbors. I started running downstream after the dogs. Someone called 911.

Our stream was lined on both sides with a tall bamboo variety called Arundinaria. It didn't severely impact the flow of the stream, especially now, but its density made it very hard to see through in most places. I raced along, hoping to find an opening, but as I ran, I realized the stream was flowing faster than I could run, and even if I could find a break to squeeze through – and even if I miraculously spotted one of the dogs – I could never swim in to make the rescue. I'd never make it out. Finally, I slowed down, trudging now, out of breath and in despair. I was three-quarters of a mile downstream.

I slowly turned around and headed back. I was too stunned to cry. We had lost our dogs, who we loved with all our hearts...all in one crazy instant. What were they thinking?! Many thoughts bounced through my head, all disastrous: Would they be trapped by a tree and overwhelmed by the huge flow, smashed against rocks, simply drowned by the speed and turbulence of the water? Would they possibly be swept out to sea, some eight miles away, and could either one survive that trip?

Would we ever find them at all?

I was trying to block out thinking about what Terryle and I would do without Gracie and Yosemite. I knew there would be way too much time for that later. We loved them so much. The enduring pain and reality would be coming soon enough. We would search, but what would be the chances of locating either one? And what relief would we get from ultimately spotting a cold, limp, battered, waterlogged carcass?

18

Our days were going to be filled with the memory of the dogs just disappearing downstream indelibly carved into our consciousness, maybe fading for a short time at some random distraction but inevitably flooding back in to be the foremost thing monopolizing our minds.

We had already been through extreme tragedy in our lives. We didn't need this, too.

As I trudged around a bend into view of Terryle and our neighbors at the crossing, I was stunned by what I saw. It looked like three golden-red dogs with the people! I rubbed my eyes and squinted. Getting closer, I could see Terryle feverishly hugging and holding two of them close. They were all wet and disheveled. My God! It was Gracie and Yosemite!

I was now running but couldn't wait to get there. I yelled, "How did they make it out?" from twenty yards away.

"It was all of a sudden," Terryle called back, "Gracie popped out of the bamboo, way down where you were running, where I could barely see her. I thought I was seeing an illusion. Gracie was shaking off the water and wagging her tail like she enjoyed the thrill! A minute later, Yosemite squeezed out, too, just a few feet from where Gracie came out."

When I got there and joined the hugging fest, I was amazed by the dogs' demeanor. They didn't seem traumatized or stunned or grateful to be alive. (Like I certainly would have been.) I swear, it wouldn't have surprised me to see them jump back in for a second round of thrills.

"That was astonishing," one of our neighbors exclaimed. "Incredible! How those dogs are here right now is a miracle. What were the chances of surviving that?! Impossible! Those two Goldens are the greatest swimmers I've ever seen."

"And for not just one but both of them to have survived," another neighbor chimed in, shaking her head. "How did they do it? It was incredible, all right! If I hadn't seen it with my own eyes…"

I was laughing through my tears.

We got them home, still stunned by the events, half-wondering if we had seen what we'd thought we'd seen. Terryle and I could barely even talk to each other; we were so shaken. We were unspeakably grateful that both dogs swam out of a situation anyone would have thought would have been fatal. It seemed like a dream.

Gracie and Yosemite acted like it was no big

    They'd forgotten about their adventure
already. Get dried off? Okay. Where was dinner?

As it happened, I was on a flight around a week later and found myself sitting next to a veterinarian. "I have a story to tell you," I said.

When I'd finished describing the incident, he said, "Yep, I'm not all that surprised; Golden Retrievers can really swim. They're bred for that, you know. Very few breeds are as good in the water. I've seen the sad sight of many a drowned dog in my day, but I've never seen a Golden drown. They can swim out of anything."

"Jeez," I thought to myself, "I sure wish I knew that a week ago."

Gracie at Christmas

Gracie and Yosemite relax after the ordeal at the stream

Terryle ("Tunes") sits by the stream watching the puppies,
George II and Yosemite

Tunes and me, circa 2000

Tunes and me, just after we met
- Photo courtesy of Michael York

Yosemite holds her toy

Gracie and her offspring, George II and Yosemite,
swim in the stream below our house

Chapter Two: Strange, Weird and Mysterious

Happiness is a warm puppy.

-Charles Schultz

Tinker and Petey 2012

"Mike, I can't talk to you right now. You wouldn't f—king believe what's happening here." I spoke these words to my buddy Mike in a tone of considerable agitation as I attempted to make it up the rocky hill, slipping and sliding, mostly crawling because it was dark, and my footing was entirely uncertain, and it felt just safer to crawl. Then, I hung up the call.

Our puppies, Petey and Tinker, were just a few months old but increasingly adventurous. This was good and bad since we lived on five forested acres, and they could roam around, run, explore, rough it a little and grow into real, outdoor-loving dogs. But they could also easily get lost in the surrounding woods if they wandered too far.

We'd already had a scary incident when Petey was just a few weeks old, and we didn't want to go through that again. He and Tinker were brother and sister Golden Retrievers, barely past the fluff ball stage, growing steadily but still small enough that they were easy prey for coyotes or mountain lions. We didn't let them stray away from the house unaccompanied, especially at night when the predators were hunting.

They were both learning to love people, as is the nature of Retrievers, but Tinker was especially social. She would say hello to anyone. A team of hooded, tattoo-faced burglars could have been sneaking toward the house with guns and knives, and she would greet them with tail-wagging kisses.

Tinker had taken to walking up the half-mile hill to our neighbors' house to say hello and hang out. She did it at least once, pretty much every day. My neighbors, Rick and Laura, were operating a bed and breakfast, so they often had new guests up there. Tinker loved everyone and, especially new people she hadn't met yet. I think her goal was to meet and greet every person in the world.

All the Airbnb guests seemed captivated by our puppy's cheerful visits, so that was OK, but she got into the habit of going up in the afternoon and did not always come back before dark. I had to hike up to get her or she'd be perfectly happy hanging with the neighbors and their dogs and horses well into the night. It was no fun trudging up the driveway in the dark, trying to find her.

This particular afternoon was the end of a trying day of editing my latest book, and I had recently finished a nice puff on a joint to unwind. That pleasant sensation was just manifesting when my wife Terryle felt she had to make an announcement.

(I might as well point out here that I've had a nickname for Terryle since we started dating: "Tunes." It was a play on the classic, old cartoons "Terry Tunes," which featured Mighty Mouse, Deputy Dawg, and others. I pretty much always called her Tunes.)

"Tinker's gone again," Tunes proclaimed.

"What do you mean?" I asked, although I knew exactly what she meant.

"I mean, she's up at the neighbors, and we have to go get her," she said, just a bit impatiently. "We can't leave her up there after dark."

Tunes says "we" a lot when we both know perfectly well that she means me.

I frowned, sighed and then went out our back door – and that meant I was hiking up the backside of the hill, along a tenuous trail among trees, shrubs and assorted natural growth – instead of going out the front door and then heading around a planted area and straight up the driveway. That was fine, I was choosing a little bit shorter way to go, but I had to watch my footing as it was getting dark. I was walking through bushes, brambles and a cluster of 100-year-old oaks, definitely a bit buzzed from the smoke. I was hiking up at an angle that would eventually connect with our driveway as it wound uphill, meeting it not far from our neighbors' house.

I was thinking, "Is this the best way to go? Is it really saving me time? Maybe I blew it on the overall decision here."

As I got closer to the driveway and the view started to open up to the valley below, I saw something that absolutely blew my mind. It was a bizarre collection of otherworldly lights at crazy angles, floating in the sky, coming up erratically toward me. I instantly had the wild thought that it was an alien spaceship flying low in the hills in my direction.

There was nobody around, so I stood and gawked as this unknown thing seemed to approach. I knew pretty much for sure that it was not a flying saucer or other interplanetary intruder – because how crazy would that be? – but it sure looked like one. I couldn't get the thought out of my head. I could not think of any other explanation.

I kept shaking my head, saying silently to myself, "That is not a flying saucer, you dummy! Really, what are the odds you'd be seeing a flying saucer all of a sudden?! Why would it be right here right now?" But the sparkling and flashing lights were getting closer; they looked really weird, and I couldn't think of any alternative.

"Holy shit, it IS a spaceship!" I gasped out loud.

I was about fifteen feet short of connecting to our driveway, stopped dead in my tracks, mouth agape. Moments later, this thing came into focus at the curve of the driveway, rounding the corner some 200 feet below where I was standing, and I could see what it really was: a fire engine! It was driving up the hill along our winding driveway, colored lights rotating on top. I'd caught different angles of the rooftop lights as they rounded and climbed curves in our road. Then, a second fire engine appeared right behind it.

"Hah!" I thought to myself, being suddenly logical. "That figures. A spaceship, c'mon!" The two fire engines were now working their way up the straight portion of the driveway. I had just been seeing odd glimpses of the pulsating lights on their roofs as the big trucks climbed out of the trees.

But then I realized that two fire engines coming up our hill at night was not a good thing. Once more, a tiny jolt of panic. I sniffed hard a couple of times but didn't smell any smoke.

The front engine was about to drive right past me, obviously heading toward the neighbors' house. I stepped back a few feet because of my utter surprise and the realization that I really did not want to talk to them. But the driver spotted me, stopped and hollered out the window, "is 9800 up there?"

"Yes," I answered, my voice squeaky with surprise that I was spotted. I cleared my throat. "Just another quarter mile up the hill. What's going on anyway?"

"Rattlesnake," he called out.

I let that information sink in and then realized that I was standing in the brush in the dark with no flashlight where I couldn't see the ground around me and anything could have been slithering up. I faintly recall that I leaped up in the air instinctively, but at any rate, I hot-footed it on tippy toes to the paved driveway. It just seemed safer.

But then it dawned on me that my puppy was up there where ten firemen were going to combat a rattlesnake! I started running behind the second fire engine and got to the house just as the firemen were jumping out of their vehicles.

My neighbors were clustered nervously on their outside deck with several people I didn't know, but I suspected they were Airbnb guests. They were talking and pointing excitedly.

"What's going on, Laura?" I asked my neighbor.

"There's a rattlesnake right down there," she said, pointing into the dark, then added for the firemen, "he's a big one. Right down there."

"Is everyone OK?" a fireman asked.

"Yes. We're up here, luckily, and it seems to be moving down the hill away from us now."

"Yeah, thcy'rc pretty shy," one of the firemen said.

"OK, good," the fireman in charge said as three or four of the crew shined lights and descended carefully. "Everyone stay here. We'll take care of it."

"What about Tinker?" I chimed in, definitely worried.

"Oh, she's fine," Laura said. "She walked up the hill to the barn around half an hour ago. She likes to schmooze with the horses."

There was a path to the barn around the front of the house, but I would have had to walk past the rattlesnake commotion to get there, so I walked across the yard and headed uphill the hard way, trudging, then crawling up the steep, unpaved backside of the slope amidst rocks, slippery dirt and brush. I could see the partly-lit barn up above, but I couldn't see my feet in the dark. This route was steep but doable in daylight, but I found out that it was way, way tougher at night.

My progress was tenuous, slipping and sliding, and I was yelling, "Tinker!" in the hopes she would just run down to me. I lit the way as best I could with my phone.

Naturally, Tinker ignored me.

About three-quarters of the way to the stables, my phone rang in my hand. I fumbled to put it to my ear but had to stop crawl-walking since I now had no light at all.

It was my friend Mike.

"What's up, Wilky?" he asked.

"Mike, I can't talk to you right now," I said. "You wouldn't f—-king believe what's happening here."

Ultimately, I made it to the top of the hill. Tinker came running, and we slid our way back to the driveway and walked down safely. We entered the house, and Tinker ran to Terryle, who hugged her and kissed her with sweet words and great affection, not paying any attention whatsoever to the actual hero of this story who had risked life and limb to retrieve her.

Tinker loves people. Here she is being held by our grandnephew, Weston

Tinker

Chapter Three: Lost Puppy

Dogs come into our lives to teach us about love;

they depart to teach us about loss.

A new dog never replaces an old dog,

it merely expands the heart.

-Author Unknown

Petey and Tinker, 2011

George Burns II was the last of our beloved threesome from Gracie's litter. Gracie, the mother of the litter, made it to 15 years old – the oldest of any of our Golden Retrievers. She swam every day even when she could barely walk to the pool, and I had to help her get there. Seeing her paddle along joyfully once she got in the water let us know she was still enjoying at least some quality of life. Gracie was a quiet marvel every day of her life and I'm more impressed than ever thinking back on her while writing this book.

Yosemite, Gracie's daughter and the sweetest, most intuitive dog we ever had, transitioned over the Rainbow Bridge when she was not quite 12. It was far too early. She had a very special bond with Tunes and was never very far away from her. In the months that Tunes was mostly bedbound with health problems, Yosemite lay down next to her and stayed all day, rising up to offer comfort whenever Tunes needed it most. Yosemite was so full of love that it erased any doubt about what an extraordinary being a dog is or why the purity of a dog's soul is so appreciated by humans. It was heartbreaking losing that sweet little girl.

George was just a real dog through and through. His canine instincts were front and center at all times. He wasn't a crazy alpha dog (like his namesake, our original George Burns, or Petey, who came later). He got along with every human and every dog he ever met. George was never a leader. He cheerfully followed the lead of his sister, Yosemite, and he was clearly lost when his sister left us.

He was just a good-natured boy and a pleasure to be around. George would let you pet him until your arm was numb and then be disappointed if you had to stop. Every day for thirteen years, when I went on my daily excursion down the hill, he was with me. The first time I walked it alone, my eyes were so full of tears that I couldn't see the way.

You feel so sorry for your dog when he passes. He won't get to chase the ball anymore like he loved to do, hike with you in the woods, swim, eat his favorite treat, or romp on the beach. But it's really not your furry friend that you feel sorry for. It's you. Because now you feel lost, and you have to somehow go on without him.

George was almost thirteen and showing signs of age. One day, when I was in Los Angeles interviewing the astounding George Adler for his biography (George was the pioneer of the off-road auto parts industry and founder of the Four Wheel Parts auto chain plus its many offshoot companies), I got a call from Tunes. She was in tears and could barely speak.

"I think our Georgie is dying," she said as best she could. "You'd better come home."

George Adler was a dog lover, and when he heard that news, he told me, "Go home, David. There's nothing more important than being with your dog when he's in distress. That's your number one priority. Go! We can get back to this any time."

Tunes and I sat with Georgie all night, taking turns petting and holding him.

I kept saying, "George Burns, good boy," in the most soothing voice I could muster.

He was sighing and groaning but certainly relaxed, buoyed up by the love we were showering him with. He didn't sleep. In the morning I took him on his last ride to the vet and came back alone.

When your wonderful, great friend is suffering and there is no joy or comfort left in his life, it is your duty to end his misery. It is one final gesture of love.

Our house was somber after that. It was the end of an era for us, the era that started with Jenny coming into our lives, the fortuitous timing of Gracie giving birth to twelve gorgeous puppies and many years of pleasure with our amazing group. It was way, way too quiet without our dogs. Something very important that we'd had for so many years, a fundamental element of our happiness, was missing.

We hosted Thanksgiving that year, and it was a nice time, although the pain of the loss of George and our other dogs was just below the surface. Most every guest commented on how quiet it seemed around our house without any Goldies racing around, wanting to be acknowledged and petted by every human. Every other time any of them had visited, there were Golden Retrievers greeting them.

Tunes and I prepared our share of the Thanksgiving food in advance, and that activity pushed the grief out of my mind, at least for a while. In cooking the turkey early Thanksgiving morning, I had a plentiful amount of excess grease. I poured part of it into a gravy mix and the remaining turkey grease into a big can, which I left on the far edge of the counter to cool. I'd learned the hard way never to pour grease down the sink.

Our guests are always great about bringing assorted dishes to make a feast and then helping to clean up afterward. This year was no different from others. After Thanksgiving dinner, some cleared plates, some wrapped up leftovers, some put away the extra table and chairs we'd brought out, and some did dishes. A couple of the guests took out the trash. When all was said and done, our house was back to normal, none the worse for the party.

A few days after Thanksgiving, Tunes and I had a heart-to-heart conversation and agreed that we couldn't get any more dogs since we were getting older and would be getting quite old, just as any young dog was coming into its own. It wasn't that it would seem disloyal to our three beloved dogs, who recently died, if we got "replacements." We never felt that way. We loved every dog for its own qualities.

Still, we'd see dogs on TV and inadvertently comment on how we missed ours. There is no dog breed portrayed more often in movies, television shows or commercials than Golden Retrievers, and we couldn't help but remark about how cute they all looked.

"Oh my gosh! Look how cute that little guy is! I wish..."

But then reality would take hold. We were not getting a dog!

One day in mid-December, Tunes summoned me into the house from my office in a little building across the yard. "Your brother's here," she called out.

"You're kidding," I replied, starting to walk over. "Which one?"

Just then, my brother George walked out of the house and waved. (I often called him "George the Human" as a tease because we had two male dogs in a row whom we named George. He pretended to be offended by that and named his son's newt Dave to get back at me. He would always make a point of introducing me to Dave anytime I visited his house.)

I gave him a hug, and we walked back in. "Come here," Tunes said, waving me into the living room. "I have something I want to show you."

And there, huddled into a box on top of a blanket, were two tiny, adorable Golden Retriever puppies.

I wanted to object, but the big smiles on Tunes' and George's faces, plus the absolute cuteness of these two puppies, drove away any inclination to reject them. I knelt down in front of the puppies, lifted them up one-by-one and completely fell in love. I felt the warmth of their bodies and the softness of their fur as I held each one against my face, inhaling the lovely and unique puppy smell, feeling the rapid little heartbeat and the involuntary squirming that they couldn't control even if they tried.

As it turned out, these puppies were only one month old. The breeder had slightly misrepresented the facts, but he drove them to George's office from over 100 miles away and delivered them to my brother. There was no going back...and these guys were so very cute.

If Tunes had figured that I would fall in love instantly and never doubt that these little beauties were home where they belonged, she figured right.

We agreed that we'd each name a puppy. I named the male dog "Petey," reminiscent of a dumb nickname friends gave me in college. (A few of them still call me that just to bug me.) Tunes named the female dog "Tinker." She just liked the name. (People asked us later if our dogs were named after Peter Pan and Tinkerbell, which they weren't, but it was so cute that we would often nod affirmatively, wry smiles on our faces.)

Petey and Tinker were brother and sister, born in the same litter in mid-November, and they were still tiny when Chanukah and Christmas came along.

We began to let them go outside, which they loved, staggering around in wonderment on their spindly, uncertain legs. But we were careful to patrol right along with them since they were vulnerable to almost any predator, including hawks, which we saw, heard and spotted in the overhead sky every single day. In those early times, I could carry both of them at once, one resting on my left arm and one on my right. They tended to scatter in opposite directions, so it was helpful to carry one while snagging the other.

We had some family over for New Year's day, and at one point, let the puppies out with us as we all enjoyed a stroll in the California sunshine. (Sorry for you, rest of the country. You've seen the Rose Parade.) Everyone was talking and laughing, and there was a little miscommunication about who was watching which puppy, but we suddenly discovered that little Petey was nowhere in sight.

We all spread out and searched the house and yard, but no one could find him. He could walk, but not very fast. Still, he was a very curious little boy, and if he wandered away, he might just keep going. He certainly would not have any idea how to get back to the house.

We started searching more desperately, walking way down and up the driveway and off into the wilderness areas that surrounded our property, calling "Petey" as loudly as we could. There was a tremendous amount of ground to cover looking for a tiny dog. How far could he have gotten?

I worked my way to my neighbors' house up the hill and asked them to keep an eye open for Petey. They immediately joined the search. As I roamed farther and farther from the driveway, I became more despondent. Tunes and I were talking every couple of minutes on the phone, but no one down below had found him, and my neighbors and I, searching the hills above our house, hadn't either.

I tried not to think of what a sad day this could be. This was the start of an entire new year. Surely, it couldn't start with a tragedy. I knew we had to search all day and all night in the hopes of finding Petey. I realized that the longer the day went on, the less chance we had of finding him. I feared that a coyote, a fox or a bobcat could grab him and disappear into the trees or that a hawk or an owl could swoop off with the defenseless puppy. Either way, we would never see him again.

We searched for over an hour and kept going. I was walking fast, desperately, covering the same ground a second time. I was yelling, "Petey!' but at this point in his young life, he didn't really know his name. I just hoped he'd recognize my voice and run into sight or at least use his tiny bark.

It started drizzling, but the rain didn't make any difference. The little guy could not have gone too far. Right? Knowing Petey, he might have even curled up and taken a nap at any time. Or...

The thought of that little guy being spirited away by a predator was a horror. Or, just as bad, wandering away somewhere and never being found, just starving or dying from the cold. I tried to keep my mind from going there, but consciously trying not to think about it caused me to think about it more than ever.

I was around a half mile from our house when Tunes called me.

"I found him!" she announced with a combination of relief and triumph in her voice.

"Thank God!" I screamed into the phone. "Where was he?"

"Right behind the house," she said. "Behind the trash cans. Somebody put a can of turkey grease back there, and he was licking away, sort of in a trance, impervious to anything else."

I ran down the hill and everyone was standing around Tunes, who was at the trash cans, holding Petey. There were big smiles all around. Sure enough, there was half a can of solidified turkey juice tipped on its side behind the trash can. I could just picture his little nose in it as he furiously licked and licked.

A helpful guest had apparently stashed the liquid behind the trash can to dry on Thanksgiving day since it would have made a mess if it were poured inside the trash. A puppy back there would not have been visible from the front, especially if he was too busy to care who was looking for him.

"He didn't hear everyone yelling for him? "I wondered out loud.

"I don't think he exactly cared," somebody volunteered, drawing a chuckle.

"He was totally focused on that yummy turkey grease," someone said, and everyone laughed again.

As a footnote, I should point out that Petey threw up many, many times that evening. Half a quart of month-old solidified turkey grease is likely to do that to a puppy.

As it turned out, this was not the first or even the most dramatic time Petey managed to get himself into a death-defying situation. Maybe we should have been more aware of what was coming.

In case you've never seen it, here is the lovely poem "the Rainbow Bridge" by Edna Clyne-Rekhy. This provides a comforting way to think of our beloved pets once they leave us...

The Rainbow Bridge

Just this side of heaven is a place called Rainbow Bridge.

When an animal dies that has been especially close to someone here, that pet goes to Rainbow Bridge. There are meadows and hills for all of our special friends so they can run and play together. There is plenty of food, water and sunshine, and our friends are warm and comfortable.

All the animals who had been ill and old are restored to health and vigor. Those who were hurt or maimed are made whole and strong again, just as we remember them in our dreams of days and times gone by. The animals are happy and content, except for one small thing; they each miss someone very special to them, who had to be left behind.

They all run and play together, but the day comes when one suddenly stops and looks into the distance. His bright eyes are intent. His eager body quivers. Suddenly he begins to run from the group, flying over the green grass, his legs carrying him faster and faster.

You have been spotted, and when you and your special friend finally meet, you cling together in joyous reunion, never to be parted again. The happy kisses rain upon your face; your hands again caress the beloved head, and you look once more into the trusting eyes of your pet, so long gone from your life but never absent from your heart.

Then you cross Rainbow Bridge together....

Edna Clyne-Rekhy

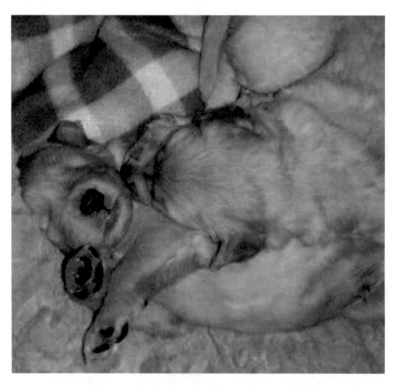

Petey and Tinker on their first day home

Tinker sleeps on top of Petey

Petey and Tinker

Tunes with me as I hold both puppies

Petey around the time when he went missing

*Despite his puppy scare, Petey loved Thanksgiving -
because he knows he's getting some turkey*

Chapter Four: The Scooter Saga

The better I get to know men,

the more I find myself loving dogs.

-Charles De Gaulle

George Burns, Gracie Allen, Yosemite, George II, Petey, Tinker 1987 – 2022

After our first dog, the beautiful Jenny, passed away, we didn't have a dog for nearly a year. I was busy flying around the country with the Pro Beach Volleyball Tour, and Terryle was revolutionizing her parents' party goods store as chief buyer and merchandiser.

This is a story that spans many years and has many interesting twists. It's a story that has some pain but mostly pleasure, especially for the dogs involved. First, though, I need to set the scene...

It is possible to get a learner's permit to drive an automobile at the age of fifteen-and-a-half in

California. I've heard that teens today are not universally eager to start driving, but young people could not wait to drive years ago when our boys, Travis and Tyler, were teens. A teen could practice any time as long as a licensed adult was with him.

Learning to ride a motorcycle is a bit different. At age fifteen-and-a-half, it's also possible to get a learner's permit to practice for getting a motorcycle license. Of course, it is not realistic to require that a licensed driver be onboard, so there was a measure of independence (and rapid transport) that young people could realize by riding a motorcycle or motor scooter.

The kids in our little town of San Clemente (in the 1980s) were all wise to that fact, and they suddenly could not bear to ride a bicycle – or, God-forbid walk – a moment longer. They begged, pleaded and nagged to get the motorized upgrade to their bicycles as soon as they turned fifteen-and-a-half. Our sons were very much in that group. Luckily, it was a request that would be fairly easy to grant.

My long-time business partner, Craig Masuoka, and I ushered in the era of professional beach volleyball a few years earlier by creating the Pro

Beach Volleyball Tour. We became aware of the popularity and potential of beach volleyball while we worked together, helping to start Volleyball Magazine. There was no professional level of the sport, although there were many great amateurs playing, and some amateur tournaments attracted nice crowds.

Our first event was the World Championship of Beach Volleyball, staged in 1976 at Will Rogers State Beach in Los Angeles. It was a huge success, and we took advantage of that to create the Pro Beach Volleyball Tour.

One of our co-sponsors was Honda Motorcycles, and I persuaded our marketing liaison to get me a good price on a scooter. I brought home that sparkling white Honda 50 cc scooter for Travis, and he was thrilled. He took off riding right away and spent loads of time scooting around San Clemente...until he turned sixteen and was able to get a car. After that, I'm not sure if he ever touched his scooter again.

Sure enough, Tyler went through the exact scenario two years later – except he wanted a black scooter since Travis chose white – and once he got a car, the scooter days were finished. Tunes and I now had two nearly new Honda Scooters to play with. And they were fun! We loved riding around the neighborhood, up into the hills, downtown or to the beach.

George Burns, the puppy version, was a high school graduation gift to Tyler from his girlfriend. Tyler immediately named him "Tybud," or Tyler's little buddy. Tybud was just a puppy and so incredibly cute, as all puppies are, and chubby, fluffy Golden Retrievers absolutely are.

But "Thai Bud" was also the name for an exotic strain of marijuana that was very popular at the time. It was supposedly from Thailand and came as dried cannabis flowers tied to a small stick.

If the puppy got outside, how were we supposed to walk up and down the street yelling "Tybud!" around the neighborhood?

Our son Tyler was given the standard parent-to-child lecture about "If you're going to have a dog, it is your job to take care of him. You'll be the one feeding him, taking him for daily exercise, and cleaning up the yard where he goes to the bathroom. Understand? We're not kidding!"

And consistent with the result of the vast majority of these lectures, Tyler agreed to the caveats but then did not follow them. In fact, he went skiing for two weeks just six days after receiving Tybud and then, three weeks later, moved out to be closer to his junior college. It was not practical to have a dog in his new apartment.

So, we inherited this beautiful Golden Retriever and all the jobs associated with having a new puppy – and thus had the unfettered right to rename Tybud, which we promptly did...to George Burns.

Full disclosure: Tunes and I hadn't had a dog since Jenny, and we fell in love with the little puppy instantly. We were not displeased the least bit to have another beautiful Golden. And George was so full of spunk and fun that he livened up our lives every day.

Now, here are the answers to a couple of questions I figure you may want to ask: Who is George Burns, and why would we name a dog after him?

Tunes adored the comedy act of George Burns and Gracie Allen. I know it's possible that many readers will not have a clue as to who they were, but they were television stars who had pioneered the transition from stand-up comedy to Vaudeville to radio and eventually to television. They were stars at every level and very funny. George Burns lived to be 100 and was still doing stand-up in his 100th year.

George (the puppy) grew into a handsome young dog with thick, red-blonde fur, streaks of blond along his chest, torso and along his rump, big paws, an appealing face and loads of energy. He topped out at a very muscular 85 pounds and, as is typical for the breed, never lost his playfulness or rambunctiousness. He didn't bark too much however, he was feisty. George loved people but was distinctly ambivalent toward other dogs. In all honesty, it is a bit lower than ambivalent. He certainly didn't like it one bit when some other dog barked at him.

I was working every day, so it was left to Tunes to take care of our young Golden Retriever, mostly single-handedly. Travis had graduated from Parsons Art Institute and moved to New York to pursue a career in art direction, and Tyler progressed to pursuing his business degree at the University of Arizona.

So it was just Tunes and George Burns at home, and they would go for long walks every day.

A few years later, I had the chance to satisfy my lifelong goal of writing fiction. Craig and I sold Surfline and my financial situation was reasonably secure. My first novel, *Big City Fish*, took 18 months to write, and it was one of the most gratifying things I've ever done.

I was working on *Big City Fish* at home every day and was able to assume the job of taking George for his daily walks. But I could see that he was not getting the exercise he really needed. Then, one day, I had a most excellent revelation. We owned two motor scooters! I walked over to the side of the house where the scooters were parked and got a big smile on my face.

I could give George some terrific exercise and have fun myself by tying a rope to his leash to add some length, fastening the leash to George's collar, attaching the now longer leash to my scooter, and scooting up and down the hilly streets where we lived. Then George could really run!

I revealed my plan to Tunes, and she was surprisingly luke warm on the idea.

"It sounds dangerous," she said.

"For George?" I asked. "He'll love it!"

"Right, no doubt about that. He's not the one I'm worried about."

I mentioned it to my friend Mike, who was a big motorcycle enthusiast, and he just laughed.

"Wilky, Wilky, Wilky," he said, "You can't be seriously thinking about doing that. That is a very big dog. Very fast, very powerful. He's not a great listener. All I can say is, be prepared to meet the pavement."

"Yeah, I know. I need to be really careful."

He just laughed and shook his head.

I thought it was a good plan. George's extended leash was rigged to be around twelve feet long, and I tethered it to my handlebar. We set out on the first day, and he was pretty confused, so it was a bit rocky. George didn't know exactly how to run this way, and we had to stop a bunch of times. But he soon figured it out and ran with me quite well. We scooted up the hilly streets every day. Mostly, he was very cooperative and ran smoothly in front of the scooter. Our rides were really fun and the high points of our days.

The hilly roads rising over San Clemente are lovely, supplying tranquil natural terrain in layers of hills – eventually giving way to mountains as the backdrop – fronted by a series of nicely designed houses, lush, beachy landscaping, pretty trees and dynamic ocean views. Our house was around two miles from the beach, but it was too low on the hill for more than a glimpse of the ocean. A nice bonus to my scooter rides with George was that the coast and ocean views I got as we went higher into the hills opened up and were gorgeous.

George and I would go up about two miles and then come back. It was uphill going and downhill coming back. We kept the speed at around fifteen to twenty miles per hour, so it was a good workout for George but not too taxing. The ride down was especially pleasant since the blue Pacific panorama was in front of us all the way.

I did have one slight complication with Georgie not being crazy about other dogs. More accurately, he would bark irritably at other dogs who barked at him and would want to confront them face-to-face. Since this was a residential neighborhood, dogs did not generally roam free. But they were often there, behind a fence, and when they saw, smelled or heard a dog (let alone a motor scooter) go by, they would usually bark. It would certainly get George's attention. It was probably his keenest focus.

When I was walking him, it was not a huge problem. I'd just tighten the leash, hold him back, and we'd walk on by. That's not so easy on a scooter with the dog tied to the handlebar. But since I knew where the barking dogs lived, I would just concentrate, speed up a little, veer to the other side of the street, firm up my grip to super tight, pull the other way if he lunged and breeze past the hazards.

This daily recreation continued for many months. I would take George every day when I possibly could. (If I was tied up with something, Tunes would take him for a walk, but she let me know she was NOT tying him to the scooter.)

"Do you think I'm crazy?" she said so forcibly the one time I suggested it that I never asked again.

Tunes also let me know that George was not thrilled by the substitution of a docile walk. He now considered a scooter run a minimum daily requirement for his mental and physical wellbeing.

One unfortunate day, we were coming down the hill from a nice ride when George saw or heard something that motivated him to veer off to the side. He changed direction with remarkable power and purposefulness. He changed direction in an instant – without giving warning to his partner in crime. He changed direction with absolutely no thought of what might happen to his buddy as a consequence of his self-obsessed decision.

Suddenly, George was bolting toward 3 o'clock, but I was still riding downhill blissfully at twenty mph or so with my handlebars pointed toward 12 o'clock. The twelve-foot safety rope was now the instrument of my demise.

Basically, George yanked me sideways so fast that the scooter did not know which way to go. It had been peacefully cruising straight downhill, so that's where the wheels had been pointing, but now the handlebars were yanked to the side, and the wheels complied. Gravity or inertia or some other evil scientific force made that scooter just slam down on its right side with me on it.

I hit the ground along with the bike, and we both tumbled over and skidded for a while. I was not hurt seriously (a grim outcome that I'm confident would have taken any amusement value right out of this story for you, the reader), but was I ever banged up. My ribs were bruised from falling onto and rolling over the scooter. Man those hurt!

Plus, it was scab-o-rama on my shoulder, knees, elbows, one eyebrow, ear and chin for two weeks.

George, to his miniscule credit, came over and licked me while I laid their moaning. I never did figure out what had caused him to change direction. My mind was not focused on diagnosing that piece of trivia. It was preoccupied with pain.

I didn't tell Mike, but he saw me a couple of days later and knew right away. He laughed and laughed very robustly and wasn't able to talk for a while. However, he did get around to it a bit later and said I should definitely keep riding with the dog tied to my scooter just for the public entertainment value.

"Don't be selfish, Wilky," he said. "Think about the rest of us. We can always use a good laugh."

Meanwhile, my wounds healed, but I was pretty gun-shy about taking George Burns on our scooter rides. For quite a while we reverted to walks, but I could see George was not getting the exercise he was used to and was not happy about the demotion. He would look at me with downright contempt. George conveniently forgot the why of our regression back to walking, although I frequently lectured him during these walks about why we were not riding anymore. He chose not to listen.

Finally, against the advice of every intelligent person I knew, I resumed tying my 85 pound dog to the handlebars of my lightweight motor scooter for rides up and down the hills of San Clemente.

This time, though, I knew the possible consequences and redoubled my efforts to be safe. I concentrated with every fiber of my ability, paying attention to every detail of our ride. It was still fun...and after a while, my tension eased...but I made sure my mind never wandered, and I never relaxed too much. This was a serious business.

And maybe George had learned a lesson, too, I speculated.

Ride after ride for month after month was so pleasant, until the ride that wasn't so great.

One afternoon I was cruising downhill with George leading the way, running fast so that I had to go pretty much full throttle on the scooter. Suddenly, George stopped. Why, you might ask? It is certainly the appropriate question. I don't know. And if George knew, he was not talking.

I successfully swerved around George in a desperation move, but – and this next part seemed to take place in slow motion – the line went almost instantly from comfortably in front of me to alarmingly taut in back of me, tied firmly from my handle bar to my recalcitrant dog...and the scooter came to an instant dead stop. As my body hurtled over the handlebars toward a painful conclusion, my mind screamed out, "Ohhhh Noooo!" Then I hit, skidded, flipped over a few times, and finally came to rest face down in the street.

Now my thoughts were being expressed out loud in something between a gasp and a groan: "Holy shit, holy shit, holy shit. Owwww! Oh, oh, oh, oh. No, no, no. Oh my God, Oh my God, Oh my God."

As the pain set in and rapidly intensified into what was going to be my new reality for the next phase of my life, I rolled over, looked blankly into the sun, had to close my eyes, and then just lay there, moaning. This was going to be bad. I just knew it. I was lying in the middle of the street, but I didn't care.

I was bleeding from the tip of my nose, forehead, cheek, ear and chin, an ankle, both elbows and both knees. My pants and shirt were torn up and blackened by the street, with blood seeping through the blackness. After some time lying in agony, I managed to stand up and stagger around for a while. The world was a white blur. Finally, I regained enough composure to roll the scooter back to the house and dumped it in a heap on the front lawn.

George came back to the house with me but kept his distance. He instinctively did not want me to assault him, although I would never do that and never had. He seemed to know, though, that there is a first time for everything.

The fact was, though, I certainly couldn't manifest my dissatisfaction with any physicality at that particular time anyway.

Tunes was quite shocked when I staggered into the house, still moaning. She insisted on taking me to the emergency room, which was a short, surreal drive for me in my condition. Miraculously, their X-rays revealed that nothing was broken. I did need stitches in my eyebrow, both knees and one elbow. And tons of disinfectant and band-aids.

The doctor felt that he simply had to lecture me. "Just exercise some common sense, for God's sake, Mr. Wilk. What is wrong with you?! Are you an idiot? You could have been very seriously hurt or even killed. You are very, very lucky, my friend. Riding a motorcycle with a dog tied to the handlebars! That is just pure insanity. Do you get that now?"

I got it! That putz didn't need to rub it in.

I didn't look too great or walk all that well for many dark days thereafter.

I had allowed myself three years to write fiction, and toward the middle of my allotted time as an author, we sold our house and moved back to Santa Barbara, our favorite city. We were able to rent a unique, airy, wooden cottage in the hills with a stream partly wrapping around it. I started a second book, *Gridlock*, and we settled in Tunes, Georgie and me.

Since this house was away from any real traffic, it occurred to me that I could take George for a run – me on the scooter and him running free, loose of any leash.

So, he was not going to be tethered to the scooter in any way! See? I learned.

I devised a route winding up into the hills on several little streets, and it was a delightful trip. There were interesting views around the canyons of the Montecito-Santa Barbara foothills with their gorgeous tall trees and a variety of home designs, some quite spectacular, all on sizeable, well-landscaped lots. We were on the wrong side of the hills to see the ocean, but we enjoyed Santa Barbara's dynamic mountain views as a backdrop. George Burns and I had fun every day.

One day George was simply not running well from the moment we left home. He wasn't limping, but he seemed very listless and stopped several times. I got off my scooter and walked over to see what was wrong when I noticed that he had two small puncture wounds perfectly centered just above his nose.

"Holy shit," I said out loud. I immediately recognized that this was a snake bite, not that I had ever seen one before in real life, but I knew right away because I'd seen this exact double puncture in movies and photos. I raced back home, called our veterinarian's emergency number, arranged to meet him at his office, lifted a very listless George Burns into the back seat, got in my car and hurried to the vet's office. George didn't even rise up to stick his head out into the wind.

(Naturally, this was a weekend because every pet disaster happens on the weekend when vet availability is low and vet or emergency clinic prices are jacked up high.)

I wish I remembered the veterinarian's name because I would give him a major endorsement here, but it was years ago, and I don't. At any rate, he met us and treated George with anti-venom, undoubtedly saving my dog's life. (George fully recovered after just a few days.) He said this was the season for snakes to be on the prowl, and he had already treated half a dozen rattlesnake bites this spring.

"May I ask you a question?" I inquired.

"Of course."

"Why would a dog stick his face close enough to get bitten by a rattlesnake that was most likely coiled and rattling?"

"Yeah, dogs always get bit on their paws or face," the vet replied. "It's because they're curious."

"You mean a dog doesn't have any built-in instinct not to get too close to a rattlesnake," I asked in disbelief.

"He does now," said the wise veterinarian.

My second book, *Gridlock*, was optioned by a motion picture development company but, as they say, stalled in development. And now, after my three-year hiatus writing books, our financial situation had gone from lovely to concerning, and I knew I needed to find a livelihood.

I had lunch with my friend and long-time partner, Craig, to seek his advice. (We worked together for Yamaha, Volleyball Magazine, and the Pro Beach Volleyball Tour and started the telephone and internet surf report Surfline).

"Pogs are coming here from Hawaii, and they're going to be red hot," he told me. "Get into pogs."

I didn't have any idea what pogs were, but I found out.

If you were a child of roughly eight to twelve during the mid-1990s or the parent of same, you remember pogs. They were a game and collectible that swept the country and much of the world for two years, then died just as abruptly as they had catapulted into popularity.

I started a pogs distributorship for Santa Barbara, Ventura and San Luis Obispo Counties, and it was a huge success. The timing was right, and sales were phenomenal. I figured I would try to sell nationally since pogs were ready to blast out of California, and I had developed a very diverse product line.

I asked my son Tyler if he would like to get involved in this effort and he did, in a very successful way. Tyler located sales companies in a dozen states and signed up a whole slate of them to represent our product line. Our orders were remarkable. We soon had the phone ringing off the hook, 17 employees wrapping and shipping orders all day, and we sold to retailers in 31 states. It was a dream come true for two years. But then the flame snuffed out as fast as it flared up. Fads and fashions that soar to instant wild popularity usually plummet right back down.

As Taylor Swift wisely said:

"You know how scared I am of elevators.

"Never trust it if it rises fast; it can't last."

She was talking about falling in love, but same difference.

Some friends had suggested that we should get a second dog to keep our first dog company. "It will keep him young," they said. And they were absolutely right. From that point on, we've always had two dogs.

We got a female puppy and named her Gracie Allen (George Burns and Gracie Allen, remember?) Getting Gracie is an amazing story in itself, and she went on to generate several other stories, including the opening chapter of this book, Swept Away. I'll be including other stories about Gracie a bit later in this book.

We moved to a new house in Goleta, California, just west of Santa Barbara. (Time out for a geographical fact. Ventura, Santa Barbara and Goleta are west of Los Angeles. People think those cities are north of LA because Highway 101 eventually progresses to San Francisco. Even the road signs read "north" and "south." But for the first 150 miles, the direction is pure west. You can take it to the bank.)

The new house was on a cul de sac with no real traffic, so it was perfect for scooter rides, which were great fun for the dogs and supplied good exercise. It was roughly a mile to the end of the block, and every day, George, Gracie and I would take a brisk trip to the end and back. No traffic, so no ropes or leashes. The dogs absolutely loved their run and looked forward to it every day.

Me too, I have to confess. It was just a lovely half hour out of the day, feeling the breeze on my face, laughing at the dogs' antics, waving to the neighbors, and enjoying the scenery.

Tragic circumstances necessitated that we move closer to the coastal city of San Luis Obispo, 100 miles to the north. I wanted to continue to maintain some business activities in Santa Barbara, so we moved to Solvang – a quaint Danish-themed tourist town located roughly half-way between San Luis Obispo and Santa Barbara.

We were able to rent a nice guest cottage on a gorgeous 150-acre cattle ranch and winery. Looking one direction, you would see a herd of 50 or so cows doing its daily grazing-meander around grassy fields. Everywhere else was vineyards. Our house was relatively isolated, and it was a nice place to be amid the heartbreak of our situation.

The route I chose for our dog and scooter run was up into the hills directly above the house along a slim dirt path. This was the first time the daily ride was on a dirt trail. A dirt bike would have been ideal, but since we only had the two motor scooters, they had to do. George and Gracie loved the run, winding around rocks and trees, ultimately climbing our way to the top of the hill, which had a dynamic view of the surrounding spread of big old oaks, cattle, lush green vineyards and the surrounding mountains.

After nearly three years, the sad situation that pushed us to Solvang was resolved, and we wanted to buy a house. We had come to really like the Solvang area and surrounding Santa Ynez Valley but simply did not have any luck finding a suitable house. Tunes searched diligently with realtors every day. We needed some land and a natural environment to heal ourselves, but we couldn't find it. Then, on a fluke, meeting friends for lunch 70 miles southeast on the outskirts of Ojai, we happened on the perfect house and bought it.

Sadly, George took his walk across the Rainbow Bridge during our time in Solvang with the early onset of cancer. He was not even ten years old. He had been a great companion over all the years and residence changes (with the exception of those scooter screw-ups). He was right by my side every day, and life was not going to be the same without him. I know that this is the cycle with pets, but the sense of loss is so very hard to bear. So hard.

When George Burns jumped into the car, as he always did, for our last car ride, it broke me.

On a positive note, though, Gracie had a litter of twelve incredibly cute puppies. We kept two – naming them George Burns Junior and Yosemite – and they grew up along with their mom Gracie in this new environment in the Ojai Valley with five acres, a pool, scores of oak trees, a lush valley backed by craggy mountains spreading out on the horizon, a stream just below us and a long, steep driveway. It was here that our three dogs all got to experience a new daily scooter ride.

By now, our two motor scooters were almost 20 years old. Although I tried to rotate them daily, they had been having assorted mechanical problems. The repair shop said they were so old that repairing them didn't make sense. I eventually had to cannibalize one for parts to keep the other one running. Still, it did run pretty well, and the three dogs and I would progress down the driveway, then ride to the end of the block where the short road terminated at a winery.

It was just short of a mile downhill to the street, then maybe a mile to the winery, then back to our driveway and uphill to the house. This was a stimulating run for the dogs, and they were pretty tuckered out by the time we got back up the steep hill. For me, it was the usual great fun.

Once day, I heard an old song that I had always liked on the radio, "Are You Ready," by Pacific Gas and Electric. It was going through my head like catchy songs do, and I adapted it the next day to our scooter ride in my loudest, proudest voice. It became:

"Are you ready – to go for your run?

Are you ready – to have some fun?

Come on, doggies, the thrill has begun.

Are you ready to go for your run?"

After a few days, I would just say, "Are You Ready?" to one or more of the dogs, and she would go crashing through the doggie door, barking with excitement. The others would always be close behind. As we took off downhill, I'd be singing as loudly as I could, and they would run in front of me really excited.

One day, one of the neighbors from down below said, "I hear you singing every morning, Dave. You have a good voice."

I don't, but we continued the ride (with my musical accompaniment) for another year until my last scooter broke down once and for all. It was the end of an era.

After that, we just walked down and back up that hill, but the dogs didn't seem to mind. They romped around together and ran up or down the hills at their whims. One would see something – often a squirrel or low-flying hawk on the prowl – and give chase, and the others would follow, barking with excitement, not knowing why but determined to participate. Meanwhile, we did our morning walk vigorously every day, and all four of us came back fatigued enough to know it was a good workout.

Petey and Tinker

Travis, a lifelong dog lover, holds the original George Burns

*My earlier career included starting the Pro Beach
Volleyball Tour with my longtime partner, Craig
Masuoka
- Photo by Rick Takagaki, Event Concepts, Inc.*

After that we started Surline, the surf report and forecast, with a third partner - Jerry Arnold - and a phenomenal employee, Sean Collins

After writing two novels, it was back into the business world and onto Pogs, a flash sensation in the mid 1990s.

Chapter Five: Going Under

Handle every situation like a dog.

If you can't eat it or play with it,

just pee on it and walk away.

- Author unknown

Petey – 2017

We share an electric gate and a long, steep driveway with our neighbors who live above us. It's just short of a one mile walk to the gate from our house, and I walk my two Golden Retrievers down, then briskly back up the driveway every morning, picking up my LA Times at the gate. I figure if nothing else happens that day, at least I got in my workout.

Off to the side, just inside the gate, there's a tiny segment of land that belongs to yet another family who has an old right-of-way to use it for grazing cattle. The cattle have miles to graze, and I almost never see them in this little patch of land right at the end of their grazing area, but maybe once every two or three years, I see some stragglers who made it that far.

This little corner of the grazing land also happens to be the location of a real-life tar pit. Yes, like the famous La Brea Tar Pits in Los Angeles.

The only reason I know there is a tar pit in that area is that one day, driving up to the gate, I was greeted by the spectacle of five cowboys dragging a large cow out of the trees toward our driveway with ropes. The cow was absolutely covered in tar up to his chest. He was being dragged on his flank from somewhere off to my right. I just sat there stunned. Who would ever have expected to see a sight like this?

"What in the world happened?" I asked.

"She got stuck in that tar pit," one of the cowboys replied, pointing off to the right. "We heard her mooing and went looking for her. Pretty surprised to see her trapped in there."

"There's a tar pit? Back in there? You're kidding. A tar pit?!"

"Yeah, right back there a ways," he said with a wave of his hand before returning to the emergency.

I watched as they laboriously pulled the cow onto the driveway and managed, with two men pulling on the rope and three lifting, to get her up to her feet. She staggered down the street, black, wet and confused, just glistening with her thick coat of tar, the cowboys walking and jogging after her.

I hiked back where he pointed and eventually spotted a black pool with leaves and wood debris floating on top.

"Damn!" I blurted out. "I've lived here 17 years and had no idea."

I couldn't wait to get up to my house and tell Tunes.

It's a very pretty walk to the gate every morning with our dogs, Petey and Tinker. There are huge old oaks all around, vistas of lovely foothills rising up to become mountains in the background, a rugged valley in the foreground, our creek down below, squirrels in the trees and many birds overhead. Now that my last motor scooter died, we walk it. It's a good workout, I often need to tell myself, especially coming back up.

Petey likes to lead the way, pushed forward by his alpha instincts. In fact, anywhere we go, he leads the way. He doesn't necessarily know where we're going; he just wants to be in front. If Tunes or I happen to veer off in another direction, he's not embarrassed or chastened. He just double-times it back to nonchalantly assume his rightful place in the lead once again, like there was never any doubt about it.

When I open the electric gate, which is in the center of a handsome and impressive long rock wall, he usually bolts out and races up the street – which luckily is a quiet dead end. I just grab my newspaper and head back uphill with Tinker. Before it slowly closes, Petey comes racing up to, of course, take the lead. If the gate is already closed, there is a gap to the side he can squeeze through.

On this particular day, the dogs were goofing around at the wall outside the gate, going wide, away from the street, in the opposite direction from where they usually ventured. They were browsing and sniffing in the bushes way over to the side of the wall as I walked inside the gate and called for them. Tinker came running. Petey lingered behind.

I was trudging up the driveway and got maybe halfway to my house when I realized that Petey

88

hadn't materialized yet. This was really odd. I got to thinking: Is there any access to that tar pit from outside the wall? It's back there somewhere. Could he work his way around the far side of the wall and get to it? Would he be crazy enough to get trapped? After a few more steps, these unlikely thoughts nagging at me, I decided to turn around.

I hate walking back downhill when I'm already walking up, but something in my gut told me I'd better take a look. Tinker just kept going toward our house. Why would she want to be inconvenienced?

I made my way a good distance through clusters of thick brush to where I could get a look at the tar pit...and what I saw was terrifying. There was Petey, up to his neck and sinking, a desperate and forlorn look on his face. Only his head remained above the tar. He could not move a muscle. And then a visibly serene look slowly transformed his face, like he accepted that he was going to die.

I panicked. Petey was somehow toward the center of the 15' by 10' tar pit as if he'd leaped after something. Maybe a bird or a squirrel. I walked around to the side closest to him and took one careful step into the pit. But I couldn't quite reach him. I took another step, leaned over, stretched out my right hand, got it under his chin and tried to pull him out. He didn't budge in the thick tar. The best I could do was keep leaning forward at this awkward angle, keep my hand under his chin and try as best I could to keep his head from sinking under.

And then I noticed that I couldn't move my own feet. And I realized that I was sinking.

Where we were was the least likely place for someone to see or hear us. We were inside the rock wall of the gate, hidden from the street, which was not heavily trafficked at all. We were set back far enough from the driveway so as to be impossible to see. But I prayed that a car would either drive by on the street or, better yet, come down the driveway from the neighbor's house. I could yell loudly enough to maybe have a chance.

My wife had a lingering illness and had not been driving. It was not going to be her to save us.

My knees were now under the tar, and I was still sinking. It was just about to my waist. I was definitely concerned, but I pushed that out of my mind because I was far more worried about Petey.

I had a way to go, but his chin was just above the tar level. Any further, and he would suffocate.

I didn't know how deep the tar pit was. Are they deep? Tar pits? I knew that countless layers of mammoths, saber tooth tigers and local dinosaurs had been fished out at La Brea. Do tar pits go ten, a hundred or a thousand feet down?

Was there any chance this one was only as deep as where we were at that moment, and we wouldn't sink any further?

If I couldn't hold him and Petey went under, I would have the unforgettable vision for the rest of my life of watching him drown in tar. That's if I even got out. At any rate, I was bent over to the point that he was right in my limited line of sight, so there was no looking away.

And then, of course, there was the matter of my own fate, which was still to be determined. It was all surreal, or, if I let my mind go there, terrifying.

Due to some little miracle, I had my cell phone in my pocket. I usually did carry it. However, it was only 7:00 in the morning and I didn't necessarily take it with me that early. The problem was that it was in my right front pocket, and my right hand was holding up Petey. To make matters worse, I was leaning so heavily forward and to the right that my pocket was not very accessible.

I reached down and over with my left hand and used two fingers to pry the pocked open. Then I worked the two fingers into my pocket and made it to the phone. Somehow, I managed to slowly work it out. There was some tar residue that had already seeped through my pants onto my phone, so it seemed I was just in time. I couldn't stand up; I was locked into this funny, odd, uncomfortable position.,

I'm right-handed, and I usually use both hands to make a call, but with my left hand, I gripped my phone as tightly as possible and, painstakingly hit 911 and then brought the phone to my left ear. Heaven forbid that I would drop the phone. I did not want to even think about that.

"This is 911. What's your emergency?" the operator asked.

"I'm trapped in a tar pit!" I screamed into the phone. "I'm going under."

"What was that, sir? I don't think I heard correctly." I quickly realized that she had never heard of an emergency like this one before.

"It's a tar pit," I repeated, trying to calm my words down a little. "It's like quicksand. My dog and I are stuck and can't get out. We're sinking! In a very few minutes, we're going to sink under the tar and die! Please, we need help fast!"

There was a tiny pause. "I'm not exactly sure what you're saying, sir, but I'll connect you to the fire department."

Luckily the line connected right away.

"Ventura Fire," a man said. "What's your emergency?

"I need help right away, please! My dog and I are stuck in a tar pit and we're going under fast. Please can you come rescue us?"

"What's that sir? A tar pit?"

"Yes!" I screamed.

"Like the La Brea Tar Pits?" His tone was incredulous.

"Yes! We're not going to last much longer!"

"What's your location, sir? We'll be there right away."

Within less than five minutes, the fire truck roared up to the gate...then continued right on by. I was screaming, but they couldn't hear me. It was not long before they hit the dead end at the edge of my block and circled back. I didn't know how soon they would return, and, believe me, it seemed like an eternity.

Finally, I heard them stop outside the gate. I yelled again as loudly as I could, "Here! Here!"

A voice shouted back, "We hear you!"

I have been glad to see firemen before, but this was by far my gladdest ever. (Ventura Fire Department, Oak View Station. This is a resounding plug for you, my friends. You guys are absolute heroes.) They came into view, eight men strong, and soon were with me. Poised on the edge of the pit, they looked at each other in astonishment.

"Wow, sir," someone said.

"This is amazing," another remarked.

"Please, help my dog," I half screamed, "he's about to go under."

"Don't worry, sir, we're going to get your dog out and you too. You're going to be fine."

"Well, please get the dog first. I, at least, have a little more time."

"Sir, we're going to get you out first. But we'll get your dog, too. You're both going to be OK."

Two firemen stepped into the shallow edge of the tar pit, put their hands under my arms, and pulled. I didn't budge. Two more stepped in, grabbed hold as best they could and I began to slowly slide out, easing vertically then horizontally as they fought the tar, pulling me toward the shallower shore.

Meanwhile, I did not take my eyes off Petey. I'd had to let go of him as they worked on pulling me out.

It took some serious pulling, but I was coming out of the tar. As more and more of me emerged, my lower torso was completely thick with tar. My socks and shoes did not make it out. (We'll be coming back to that little detail a bit later.) The firemen carried me to a nearby tree and sat me down against it. I just sat there, stunned. Not yet happy, not even relieved, just utterly stunned.

Looking out at this unbelievable scene, random thoughts started to invade my brain. Imagine if I hadn't gone back to look for Petey at the time I did. Or if I just hadn't checked the tar pit? He would have disappeared under the surface of the tar, never to be seen again. We would have looked frantically, driven around for hours and days calling his name, talked to all the neighbors, reported him missing to the animal shelter, called them every hour or so, circulated word on social media...

We would have never found him or had any idea of his fate.

My God! Imagine if I had disappeared too.

Since Petey was in so deep, they couldn't step in to grab him. They would have all ended up like me. They shouted instructions back and forth, and two men went back to the firetruck and pulled off a ladder. They came back, and three of them laid the ladder across the tar pit. It went right next to Petey and was long enough to reach the solid banks on both sides. It was pretty much covered with tar in the middle, but it created a solid surface.

A fireman crawled out, reached down and tried to pull Petey by his head, the only part of him not submerged. Of course, Petey didn't budge an inch. The fact of the matter is, his big Golden Retriever head would have popped clean off before he would have come out of the tar. Tar pits, as it turns out, are darned thick.

Another fireman handed the first man a shovel, and he began shoveling tar away from the area right next to Petey. It was very difficult shoveling, but he slowly made progress. Several firemen brought out a second ladder and laid it next to Petey on his other side. Then, a fireman walked out on the ladder and started shoveling from behind him.

The rescuers were largely covered in tar by now and their ladder and shovels were pretty much saturated in the thick, awful, Sulphur-smelling stuff.

After a while, they had shoveled enough tar away so that one fireman could push a rope under Petey's torso far enough for the other man to feel it and pull it the rest of the way. Then they did it again to double it up. With a rope under Petey, six firemen, three on each solid bank, started pulling. It looked amazingly difficult, but slowly, Petey started to emerge.

I was bug-eyed looking on.

Finally, they pulled him out, twice as thick as usual due to the solid several inches of tar covering every part of his body. He shook, as dogs do when they are wet, but nothing came off. He walked away from the tar pit gingerly and stood confused, not quite halfway to the driveway.

Dogs quite often act a little dazed and confused, if you know what I mean. Or maybe it's more accurate to say that they are just totally ensconced in their own dog mentality and not in tune with human consciousness. They're always in the now, with little regard for the future.

At any rate, Petey, more than ever, did not know what to think.

"Sir, we need to take you to the hospital," one of the firemen told me.

"No, I think I'm going to be all right," I said. "Thank you SO MUCH for saving our lives. You guys are incredible! We would have both disappeared without you!"

"But I need to figure out how to get the tar off my dog."

(I started to have an inkling of what a monumental task THAT would be.)

"Yeah, you need to get him to a vet or an animal hospital," one said.

But I was already figuring that was not going to be possible. My car would be ruined forever if I put him inside, and it would take the vet's full staff all day to get Petey clean. They had other things to do.

Me walking into their office with a Golden Retriever covered in tar was the last thing they ever, ever wanted to see.

While the fireman began the unenviable process of trying to get their pants, boots, ladders and shovels a bit more presentable by pouring kerosene over everything, I started trudging up the driveway behind my tar-covered dog. He had, of course, taken the lead.

(The "I lost my shoes and socks" part starts here.) To make matters worse, I am a tenderfoot, and it was rough trudging up the blacktop driveway barefoot. It was "ooh-ow" with every step. There is an amazing amount of pebbles, rocks, acorns and twigs on my driveway. You don't really notice it until you walk on it barefoot. You can try to avoid stepping on the worst ones, but that just lands you with less balance straight onto the second worst ones.

You would think that maybe having tar coating your feet might bring a tiny reprieve from the stings and pings of the penetrating pain, but it is vastly inferior to any kind of shoe for protection.

Still, being realistic, my troubles before and after this walk were so immense that I am embarrassed to even mention these 10 minutes of torture.

It is only in reverence to good journalism that I even do.

I tried to anticipate, as I trudged up the hill, what it would be like to get Pete clean. But my projection failed to even come close to the misery of the next many hours.

I got up to the house, screaming at Petey NOT to go in the doggie door. Not only did that not work, but he went in, came back out, then went in again...and came back out again, confused by my yelling. I was tenderfooting it up to the back door as fast as I could but not moving all that fast. The result was one unbelievably tarred-up doggie door...but at least he hadn't trekked very deeply into the interior of our house.

"Tunes!" I hollered, sticking my head inside the door.

"Where have you been? Tinker came back half an hour ago. I was starting to worry...what in the world!" she gasped. Tunes was way surprised to see the two of us standing outside the door forlornly covered in...tar? Surprised doesn't actually do justice to the look on her face. But what word would?

Tar Pit Terror (part II)

So, unfortunately, this story is far from over.

We knew from visits to the beaches in Ventura and Santa Barbara how to get little smears of tar off our feet. You simply rub the tar off with baby oil and paper towels. And we had a bottle of baby oil and a few rolls of paper towels. But to hope those would do the job proved to be woefully naive. What we had on hand fell way, way, way short of what would be needed.

I peeled off my tar pants and underwear and threw them in the trash bin. I put on some clean pants, socks and shoes that Tunes brought me and set up a square yard or so of collapsed boxes near our back door for Petey to stand on while we worked on the tar. No sense getting clumps of tar all over the porch and driveway...which we did, somehow, anyway.

Tunes started to work on Petey while I raced to the nearest sizeable drug store to buy baby oil and paper towels. I bought out all their stock – eleven bottles of baby oil and nine eight-packs of paper towels – and raced home.

I drove home hoping that Tunes would have gotten Petey somewhat clean by the time I made it back, but that aspiration met with bleak disappointment. In fact, I didn't notice any progress whatsoever. Petey was completely covered in tar before and after my trip. Our one bottle of baby oil was empty, and the few rolls of paper towels we'd had at the house were covering the ground, two hundred crumpled-up sheets saturated in tar.

"This is not going to be easy," Tunes remarked, forlornly.

We realized that we needed to clear Petey's genitals, or he would not be able to relieve himself. We couldn't even see them at the moment; we had to kind of guess where they even were. It took an hour just to clear those at all adequately.

The best technique for removing the tar was to saturate one spot on his body with a major squirt of baby oil, then use a few paper towels to scrape off whatever tar would come. (It simply would not come off unless thoroughly doused first.) It was obviously going to take a huge load of paper towels, even though each one we used became totally covered in tar. After a few hours, all the baby oil and paper towels were gone, and Petey was far from spotless.

So I jumped in my car, and headed to another drug store in the opposite direction and bought out their stock of baby oil and paper towels, too. I also had an inspiration: Dawn dish soap. That's what the wildlife rescue people used on birds and sea mammals that got covered in oil from ocean oil leaks. I bought every bottle they had, which was seven.

By seven o'clock, Pete was a lot cleaner but far from tar-free. We knew that he would try to lick it off, just out of instinct. But that would poison him and had to be avoided. Tunes found an old dog neck cone (we call it a radar dome) in the closet and got it ready for later.

I took him over to the hose, loaded him up with many squirts of Dawn, and lathered him up really well. When I rinsed it off, it had made a difference. I repeated the process eight or nine more times while Tunes got a rest, then brought him back for more baby oil treatment.

It was no fun doing this. Tunes and I were on our knees for many hours, and our legs and backs were killing us. By some miracle, Petey was pretty good about the ordeal. He only ran away a couple of times, but we managed to get him back. Maybe Petey sensed that he was (we were) in crisis, but he stood there passively for all those hours and let us do our thing, trying to get the tar off.

Tinker came outside from time to time to observe the scene with a miniscule degree of interest. She walked around us, assessing the situation, at no point volunteering to help, and then sauntered back into the house each time, the doggie door closing with a slap.

By 9:00 at night, we couldn't do it anymore. Pete still had plenty of tar on him, but we'd gotten eighty percent of it off. We had to let him come into the house and fitted him with the protective cone collar so he couldn't lick off any remaining tar. We put an old white sheet over Petey's dog bed to try to preserve it. The sheet did the job, but it was as destined for the trash as anything you've ever seen.

Then we scrubbed our hands and arms and collapsed into bed.

By 7 a.m., we were back at it. I started with half a dozen Dawn shampoos. We spent a few more hours on baby oil treatment. I gave Pete four or five more Dawn shampoos...and he was pretty damn clean. He looked like a dog again.

He was prancing around, acting normally, like nothing had happened the past two days. His memory is annoyingly selective, so I'm sure he completely forgot.

But he did seem to remember not to go anywhere near that tar pit again. Meanwhile, to be certain, we fenced it off.

Around a week later, I was driving near the Oak View Fire Department with the dogs in the back seat. So I stopped, let them out, and walked in to thank the crew again while the dogs raced around, tails wagging furiously, greeting everyone. The fire crew all remembered our ordeal and said it was the craziest thing they'd ever seen. They put it on their Facebook page, and it got hundreds of likes and comments. Of course, I thanked them profusely and shook everyone's hand. They had saved our lives, no doubt about it.

So, I was trying to think of a moral of this story, which is not easy, but this is what I came up with: if you happen to have a tar pit near your property, DO NOT let your dog get anywhere near it.

Chapter Six: The Bear

A true friend leaves pawprints on your heart

-Author Unknown

George Burns II, 2011

This is a story about the vital importance of watchdogs.

Summer days are hot in the Ojai Valley, sometimes getting up into the high 90s or occasionally over 100 degrees. It was a definite challenge to keep it as cool as possible inside the house while using as little air conditioning as we could. If we didn't, our electric bills would be swoon-worthy.

But luckily, it usually cooled off into the high sixties or even lower at night, so we developed a drill I called "eight to eight." Basically, I opened all the windows at around 8 p.m. (sundown, essentially) to take advantage of the cool evenings and closed them at 8 a.m. just as the day was heating up.

If it was a particularly hot day, I would open the front door, too, at sundown to maximize circulation and let even more cool air into the house.

This story happened on a mid-summer evening several years before the tar pit drama after the magical Gracie and our sweet Yosemite had already made their way over the Rainbow Bridge. Georgie Burns II was our only remaining dog, and he was twelve.

George had been a good watchdog (for a Golden Retriever, if you know what I mean) in his earlier days and with his bulk, he appeared to be a real force. He would bark long and loud at intruders and intimidated many a visitor who ventured up to see us. Little did they know what a sweet boy he was and that he was only barking out of eagerness to greet someone with big, wet kisses. He wouldn't bite anyone unless they rubbed their body down with steak juice.

Visiting dogs were quite respectful of the large Goldie, although he was no threat at all. The occasional coyote who ventured into view turned and ran at the sight of the big fellow.

But now, in his thirteenth year, George's energy level was much dissipated. His hearing was shot, and his powerful running stride had slowed to a trot. Nevertheless, George was a big, lumbering sweetheart and as loyal as they come. We loved him dearly.

This particular evening, I was watching a baseball game on TV in the living room while Tunes was working on some crafty project in our bedroom. It was right around sundown, and I had just opened the front door.

The last I'd seen of George, he was asleep just out of sight at the edge of the kitchen, perhaps ten feet away.

I couldn't quite see the front door from where I was sitting, and the first few feet into the house were further obscured from where I was by the dining room table. I looked up casually between pitches to see just the top of a dark form walking into the house. I figured it was George, but it was odd that I could see his back over the dining room table. George was tall, but not that tall. Also, the dog entering the house seemed a darker color than

George's red/golden hue. But the light was fading, and I didn't give the whole thing much thought in that very first instant.

But all that changed a moment later when the creature's giant head emerged into view. He looked right at me. It was a black bear! Walking into our house! I looked at the bear in shock. What was he doing in my house? The shock temporarily numbed the sense of fear that was going to come at any moment. Good reasoning, as in what I should do next, was still warming up in the bullpen.

Later, I figured that the bear was not fully grown, but he was still big, perhaps 250 or 300 pounds. Bigger than me, bigger than George, bigger than both of us combined. Also, the ramifications of a bear in the house became much clearer in retrospect. He could have attacked Tunes or me, ransacked the house, tore through the kitchen...or if he went after George, who was sleeping less than fifteen feet away from him, it could have been a terrible scene. But I did not have time to think about all this in the heat of the moment.

I leaped up instinctively, yelled and ran toward the bear. Now, this was, at best, stupid and could have been disastrous. My impulsive reaction really did not hold up in any kind of calm analysis later on. But I got lucky, and things played out about as well as they possibly could have. The bear instinctively backed up slowly as I approached – I guess he was alarmed by my sudden freakout – and continued walking backwards right back out the front door.

I looked on in astonishment as he slowly and casually rambled across the yard toward the forest on the fringe of our property. He never looked back at me.

I called out frantically to Tunes.

"Tunes! Get in here right away. You have to see this!" She came running in and got a chance to see the bear before he disappeared. This was important in retrospect because if she or anyone else questioned my credibility – which has somehow been known to happen – I had a witness. In a moment, the bear was gone. Tunes was amazed when I told her the full story.

And (here's the watchdog part) to his everlasting credit, George woke up not ten minutes later, raised his head, looked around suspiciously, sniffed the air...and barked one single, emphatic, disapproving bark: "Woof!"

Chapter Seven: Devastation

When the world around me is going crazy

and I feel like I'm losing faith in humanity,

I just have to look into my dog's eyes

to know that good still exists.

-        Author Unknown

{George Burns, Gracie Allen 1996}

It was early morning when the phone rang.

Although it was fall, it was a lovely day. The sun had risen not an hour before, and early sunshine was streaming in through the windows all around the front of the house, making it bright and cheerful. Outside, the orange trees sparkled with a silvery glow, their morning coat of dew lit up at a perfect angle by the sun.

I was already up making coffee, so I walked over and lifted the phone out of its cradle on the edge of the kitchen. It was the most terrible news of our lives.

The voice on the other end identified himself as a police officer with the San Luis Obispo Police Department.

"Are you David Wilk?" he asked.

"Yes."

"Do you know a Terryle Wilk."

"Yes, she's my wife."

"And do you know a Tyler Hutchison?"

"Yes. He's my son. What's going on?"

"Sir, I'm afraid I have some very bad news to report to you. Your son Tyler has been killed."

"What?! (Pause) Wait, what did you say?"

"Sir, Tyler Hutchison has been killed by a gunshot wound. It happened the night before Halloween. We need you and your wife to come up to our office to get all the details. You can arrange to view the body at that time if you wish."

Terryle overheard my tone of voice and shouted out for me to tell her what was wrong.

I walked down the hall toward the bedroom, which seemed 100 miles away. My ears were ringing. My body felt hot, but at the same time, I was numb all over and didn't feel like I was in my body. I don't remember breathing. Was I going to pass out? It was like I was in a horrific, awful dream. Yes! Please let this be a dream.

Have you ever known that you were about to announce something that another person does not expect, but it's going to change their life? One moment you know it and the other person doesn't yet and things seem outwardly normal, but you also know this huge wrecking ball is coming, and it's going to ruin everything.

I knew that what I had to tell Tunes was going to be a life changer. I knew it, but never imagined it would be so much worse than I thought.

I stood next to the bed lamely, cleared my throat and told Tunes that Tyler had been killed.

She cried out in one single shriek that was the most anguished, unforgettable, heartbroken sound I have ever heard.

"No!!!"

This was the beginning of a heart-crushing nightmare that haunts us to this day. It also triggered a series of events over the next several years that were almost entirely horrible.

We made the 90-minute drive to San Luis Obispo pretty much in stunned silence that afternoon. What could we say? We were ushered into the two-story downtown police department and taken into a private room where we were joined by two officers. There was no doubting how affected we were by the news. An officer cleared his throat and began.

"Your son Tyler Hutchison was with his friend Mark at his home in Avila Beach on the night of October 29th. They were drinking together late at night and started fooling around with a new pistol that Mark had acquired. Just after midnight, Tyler accidentally shot himself in the head with Mark's gun. It was instantly fatal."

He probably said more than that, but that was the gist of it.

The San Luis Obispo Police Department had apparently been in Santa Barbara trying to reach us for several days (we had moved a few months before), but the accident had taken place almost a week earlier. It was still under investigation, and they would provide more details as the investigation progressed. They had notified Tyler's birth father, Bill Hutchison, that day as well.

Once we got home, Terryle collapsed on the bed, sobbing, while I made a couple of excruciating phone calls, and the shocking news began to spread. Friends and family rushed to console us and help us try to cope. It helped, I imagine, the loving support, but the unparalleled grief was not going away.

They assisted in organizing a celebration of life at our home because, frankly, we were not capable of that. Several dozen of our friends, family and Tyler's friends attended. It was a somber and surreal event. As the liquor flowed, the mood elevated a bit, but it was artificial. The pain was going to be there long after the guests left.

It was a pretty day, mostly sunny and reasonably warm for fall weather, when the gathering started next to a lovely little rock-themed pool behind the house we were renting. Directly behind the pool was a small orchard of healthy orange trees and off to one side were twelve avocado trees. On the other side was a section of lawn. We greeted everyone with hugs and tears. People didn't know what to say.

Tyler was just 25 when he died. I said a few words about his life. I hadn't prepared any speech, but I'd known Tyler since he was five, and he grew up with his mom and me. I talked about Tyler's upbeat attitude toward life, his relentless positivity, his charm and magnetic personality. His smile. I talked about Tyler's success playing sports throughout his life and his continued dedication to staying in shape. I told the story of how much he'd helped me in my Pogs business, showing real acumen for sales at such a young age. I have no doubt that Tyler had a great future ahead of him.

Tyler's brother Travis flew in from Berlin, where he had been living the past few years. He was staggered by the news about his brother and elected not to speak. Tyler's father, Bill Hutchison, was there, but he was a shadow of himself, so torn up that he couldn't say anything. He and Tyler had a very special bond. Tyler's Uncle Brian spoke, too, simply but elegantly, fighting off the tears. Tunes' father, my dad and two of my brothers said brief words.

Several of Tyler's friends spoke about his strong points, memories together, sense of humor, and how special their friendship was. Most of them faltered as tears choked their voices. Tyler's friend Mark, the person who had been with him at the time of the accident, attended the event with his family. He seemed heartbroken. It was his gun, and we all sympathized with him. Of course, he didn't speak to the gathering.

Our dog George lightened the mood as much as was possible. Being a Golden Retriever, he made sure to greet every single person, stick with them as long as the petting was robust, and then move on to the next customer. It was exciting for George to have so many people around. He certainly didn't mind gobbling a few snacks if they were being offered. Georgie seemed to be everywhere, and his good nature was appreciated. Tyler's friends remembered him as a puppy and called him "Tybud."

The celebration of life helped dull the pain, but for us, there was the next day to deal with and all those days afterward.

A week later, the district attorney for San Luis Obispo called. We were stunned by what he told us. The case was now being investigated as a murder. There was a lot of new evidence pointing that way. We needed to come up right away to discuss all this.

The district attorney was an impressive man in his early forties. He was tall and handsome in his nicely-pressed, dark grey suit. His face wore a sympathetic look. He spoke like a sad friend. He told us that Mark had not reported the shooting for three days.

"Police investigators discovered that during that time, Mark crammed Tyler's body into a dumb waiter," the DA told us, "then he dropped Tyler into the garage, went downstairs and covered him up with a blanket. Mark rented a carpet shampooer and meticulously cleaned up the apartment so there were no visible traces of Tyler's blood. When detectives checked Mark's gun it had been thoroughly wiped of all prints."

I was stunned, eyes opened extra-wide, barely breathing, not even wondering if speech was possible. I held Terryle's hand and no doubt she was reacting the same way.

"Mark canceled a get-together with friends that he and Tyler had organized for the weekend," he went on. "He told several people that Tyler had suddenly decided to go to Las Vegas instead and had left town.

"Tyler's car was found by the Los Angeles Police Department in a rough neighborhood east of L.A. International Airport – 200 miles away. We're wondering how it got there. Mark says he has no idea. Just coincidentally, the windows were down, and the keys left in the ignition, so somebody was obviously inviting someone to steal it. But amazingly, the car was perfectly intact."

Terryle and I asked a few questions. The district attorney had some answers but not the important answers. Mark and his attorney were not saying much at this time.

"Mark attended a party in town two days after the shooting," he continued. "He had a few drinks, talked to friends, danced and acted normally. We have this verified by two other people who were there. Meanwhile, Tyler's body was lying in the garage the whole time, stuffed into the dumb waiter.

Terryle gasped and sobbed.

"After three days, Mark, his parents and a prominent defense attorney went to the police station to report the 'accident.' Mark claimed he had been in shock and crying non-stop and could not function for the longest time. He said he couldn't remember all the clean-up and going to the party and the other things he did in the aftermath of the shooting. He claimed that he was in such a fog that he must have been doing all that on auto-pilot.

"Finally, he went to his parents, told them the horrible news, and they rushed to the police station. Somehow, they picked up a very capable criminal attorney on the way...briefed him thoroughly...and he did most of the talking."

The district attorney told us that no one believed Mark's story. Why had he gone to such considerable efforts to cover everything up instead of reporting it as an accidental shooting right away? How did Tyler's car get to the LA Airport area? Why did Mark attempt to hide any traces of blood and lie to so many people about where Tyler was before revealing Tyler's death?

"Tyler's body was wedged into the dumbwaiter so firmly," the DA told us, "that it took three policemen several minutes to pry and yank him out. We figure that Mark would have disposed of Tyler's body, but he couldn't physically get it free. He had no choice but to ultimately report it to the police."

In the next few weeks, other details of the heartless cover-up came to light.

Tunes and I were in such a low place that it was unfathomable. We couldn't think, barely talked, and never seemed hungry. We were in a daze. The days dragged on endlessly. And now frustration and anger with Mark's suspected murder of our son were very much in the equation.

We had periodic meetings with the DA. A few of Tyler's friends told us ugly stories about what a reckless character Mark was, and we urged them to tell everything to law enforcement in San Luis Obispo.

A date for the murder trial was set, but it was many months away. The trial seemed like the only thing we had to look forward to, but how terrible do things have to be for THAT to be what you're looking forward to?

The truth is, we were in limbo, stuck, frozen into depression. Tunes' health began to collapse as well.

I happened to overhear a conversation between two young people, a boy and a girl, standing in line at a retail store sometime in mid-December. The young lady mentioned that a family they both knew had just had a litter of Golden Retrievers. They were adorable, the sweetest puppies she'd ever seen.

I walked over and apologized for interrupting.

"My name is Dave Wilk," I told them. "I overheard you guys talking about some Golden Retriever puppies. We love Goldies. They're our favorite dogs."

I cleared my throat. "Our family has just been through a horrible tragedy," I said. "Our son was murdered a few weeks ago. We're so depressed we don't know what to do with ourselves."

The teen girl and boy listened with increasingly shocked expressions on their faces.

"I'm wondering if, by any chance, any of those puppies are still available? Maybe getting a beautiful puppy will lift our spirits a tiny bit. I promise we'll give the puppy a warm, loving home."

"I think all the dogs are spoken for," the girl replied in a sad, sympathetic tone. "I'll be glad to ask the family and let you know."

I told her how much I would appreciate that.

Later that day, the young lady called and said the puppies were all committed, but considering what we were going through, the family was giving one up that they intended to keep, and we could buy it if we wished.

I rushed over to the house and met the owner. She was so nice, so consoling. I saw the puppies playing in their pen in the garage and met the one small, scrawny, pink female that could be ours if we wanted. I said yes, absolutely.

The puppies were still tiny, not even one month old. I had never seen a puppy that young. They were only just developing the thick, fuzzy blonde fur that made this breed so adorable. I was able to hold our puppy, and she was very sweet. She was not the prettiest, biggest or most lively puppy in the litter, but that didn't matter.

As it turned out, she was incredible.

The puppies were too young to go to their new homes yet, but the family let me bring ours home to be with us on Christmas day. Our new puppy staggered around the Christmas tree a bit, but she had so little stamina that she fell asleep several times. She would literally fall asleep and collapse while walking. Still, when she was awake, she gave nice kisses. Tunes held her in her lap for many hours. She would not let go. She didn't want me to take the little girl back to her mother until she was old enough to adopt, but I had promised.

A few weeks later, we were able to bring our puppy home for good. Since we had George Burns already, we named her Gracie Allen.

There is no doubt in my mind that little Gracie saved our lives. Her sweetness, puppy innocence and playfulness were the one positive focus of our daily lives. If constant attention and hugging and kisses can spoil a puppy, then Gracie was as spoiled as they get.

Chapter Eight: The Trial

Dogs are not our whole lives,

but they make our lives whole

-Roger Karas

Gracie, George Burns 1999

George was a little put off by his new sister at first, growling at the intruder, nipping a bit when she annoyed him, and letting Gracie know on no uncertain terms who was boss. He towered over her like a giant. But she persisted after him, and after a while, he would let her crawl on his head, nip his ears and jump around trying to get him to play with her. He pretended not to be, but George grew really fond of Gracie.

After just a few weeks it was obvious that she was the more active of the two, always getting into something, loving to explore the house and yard, bouncing along in a funny puppy trot, endlessly curious. If we left pretty much anything on the floor anywhere in the house, Gracie would find it and chew it, guaranteed. Sometimes, you could hear her but not see her. That meant she was behind something or under it – places she should not have been – but she was blissfully ignorant of protocol and endlessly curious. George was an active boy, but he never really matched her energy or ambition.

One thing he did get to do that Gracie was too small for was to join our daily run with the motor scooter. I had to keep Gracie inside because she would always run after us, despite me proclaiming loudly in my most serious tone, "No!" and "Gracie, You Stay!" From an early age, Gracie did not appreciate being told no.

Adoration for our dogs bought us a little break from the haunting sadness of knowing our son had been murdered. Tunes' health spiraled downward, and she descended into a cycle of profound medical problems that never went away. Her legs and feet developed extreme pain that made it almost impossible to walk. Her head, back and shoulders hurt from tension. Suddenly, she was getting migraines. Tunes ground her teeth almost constantly and threw up almost every day, loosening her teeth and ruining her enamel. Her stomach churned and hurt, which ultimately led to many surgeries. She had extreme nausea that sometimes lasted all day. Amazingly, despite all that, she was still beautiful.

And, of course, her emotions were overwhelming. Tears would come often, and sometimes they wouldn't stop. We were seeing a therapist together and continued for several years. It helped me more than Tunes.

One night, our scruffy little puppy Gracie was with us in our living room, and I pulled out a little red wiffle golf ball I'd picked up in town. I let her sniff it, then handed it to her, and she immediately started chomping on it. I took it back, which was not easy, and rolled it across the carpet.

Gracie romped after it right away, pounced on it, tossed her head around for a while (like she had caught a very miniaturized rabbit), then laid down, chomping it proudly. After considerable urging, Gracie warily brought the ball, and I was able to get it away from her. I rolled it again and she soon realized it was a game and much enhanced if she brought the ball back. She was a natural ball chaser. Little did we know that we were creating a monster. Gracie would bring the ball back and insist on another throw and another and another...endlessly. If I wasn't being responsive enough, she would take the little ball over to Tunes.

Gracie never wanted to stop...and that became a lifetime characteristic.

I walked over to the front of our carpeted staircase one evening, ball visibly in my hand and the puppy eagerly following. I tossed the ball up a few steps, and Gracie went right up after it, as best she could, with no coaching. It wasn't easy for her because the stairs were almost as tall as she was, and Gracie had to rise and plant her front paws at the bottom of each new step, then leap up and claw and struggle her way up that one and each progressive step. It took several seconds per step. I had to laugh. Her determination, though, was impressive.

"Honey, come over here and watch Gracie," I called to Tunes. "You've gotta see this. It's hilarious."

I started with three stairs up. Gracie did her thing, and Terryle wanted the next throw. It was fun trying to throw it perfectly so it did not hit the back of another step and roll back down. You had to loft it softly to bounce at the front end of a stair so it could roll forward, but your touch had to be perfect. Tunes and I took turns tossing the ball up a few stairs, going a bit higher with time.

Gracie clambered up each stair, snagged the ball, then plopped her way back down each step triumphantly for an encore. It was so amusing to watch. The height of the stairs didn't stop her. Gracie showed the single-minded focus that she manifested all of her life. When she set out to do something, there was no deterring her.

After a couple of weeks, I had an inspiration and tossed the ball up onto the balcony above the stairs. Gracie ran, jumped and clawed her way up to the balcony, got the ball, and then stood victoriously with her head through the railing, looking down, posing, showing us that the ball did not and was never going to elude her. We didn't expect that, but it sure had us laughing.

This became the game because it would take her a few minutes per ball chase, clamoring up all those steps, strutting for a while, then loudly half-tumbling back down, buying us a bit of a break. Tunes and I would take turns making the throw to extend the break even further, and we could half-watch something on television at the same time.

When we finally decided it was enough, Gracie was never happy.

Those interludes were so normal and blissful that they were extremely important to our slim hold on keeping it together.

When the trial got underway, it was certainly no relief. Our close friend and personal attorney, David Turpin, helped us prepare, interfaced with the district attorney, and attended the trial as often as he could, although the DA handled the prosecution.

The courthouse was on the edge of downtown San Luis Obispo, a blocky, respectable building, but not ornate or fancy. To the side of the steps up to the courthouse was a handsome square pillar with a small light tower on top. On the pillar was the inscription: San Luis Obispo, County Courthouse, 1940.

The steps led up to a small plaza with lawns and bushes to the sides of a sidewalk leading into the building. The main courthouse was two-story, fronted by a thin, three-story, carpeted entry that also accommodated some of the court offices.

Directly ahead as we walked in were wide, carpeted steps leading to the "action" floor, where the courtrooms were located. Our courtroom was the last one down the hallway to the right. It was one of two superior courts for criminal cases.

We walked into the courthouse the first day, feeling an unsettling mixture of hope and uncertainty. We expected the trial to progress to a guilty verdict and somehow bring some small measure of relief to our nightmare, but we didn't know what kind of an elevator ride the trial would be. Tunes and I had not been able to talk about it very much. We just couldn't. Our pain and our thoughts about what the trial would be like were individually internalized. We held each other more than ever at home, but our conversation level was much reduced.

For me, my experience with courtroom drama was drawn from movies and television. That sounds ridiculously naïve, but I had certainly never attended a murder trial in person. The actual process is excruciatingly meticulous and tedious – nothing like TV. It is not fun, and it is not the least bit entertaining.

Several friends and family members attended the trial with us that first day. A large crowd of locals gathered to see the trial as well as spectators. Mark's family was very well known in San Luis Obispo, and the case had gotten a ton of media coverage in the region. The courtroom had a capacity of roughly 150, and quite a few people who showed up did not get seats in the austere, wood-paneled room that tried to be elegant but didn't quite succeed.

The courtroom was laid out into two seating sections with an aisle in between. On the left side (as you faced forward) was a table at which the defendant and his attorney sat. The defendant, Mark, was a tall, well-built, good-looking young man with medium-length brown hair and no facial hair, dressed this first day in a short-sleeved shirt and beige slacks, casual but nice clothes. His attorney was a slightly frumpled older man, wearing a dark suit and perpetually fidgeting with one thing or another on his table.

Behind them, in the first row of seating, were Mark's mother, stepfather and sister. A few other family friends and "supporters" sat next to and in the row behind them.

The right side was fronted with the District Attorney's table, with the DA, another attorney from their office and their chief investigator seated left to right. There was room for our attorney on the days he attended. San Luis Obispo's district attorney, with whom we'd met several times, had a nice smile and an easy manner. He was very consoling to us, and we liked him a lot.

In front of the tables was a wide space, and then the middle-aged, female court reporter seated in front of the judge. Behind her was a handsome podium for the judge, with short wings on both sides for documents he referred to from time to time. Next to him was the witness box, where witnesses paraded in to testify after being escorted by the court bailiff. The bailiff stood or sat on a high chair off to the side when not active. To the far right side, in a two-row set of seats that was elevated like bleachers, sat the jury.

Opening day was mostly procedural, so not much happened. By the second day, our friends and family were depleted, but the crowd was still near capacity. We had no idea what a long ride this was going to be. Day after day, we did the same thing: walked up the steps to the second floor of the

133

courthouse and trudged down the hall to the courtroom, sighing as we entered and taking our seats, preparing for a stressful, tedious day. There were a couple of merciful breaks and 90 minutes for lunch, then more of the same stress and tedium.

As the actual trial process got underway, jury selection and other procedures dragged on. The prosecution's case is presented before the defense, so at least we began the ordeal hearing the testimony that felt like the truth. Still, it was necessary to introduce a great many photos of Tyler's dead body in grim condition, close-ups of his head exploded by a bullet, plus photos of the gun, the cleaned house and Tyler's car stranded four or five miles east of Los Angeles International Airport. These were all effective, but so distressing for us to have to view. For the most part, we looked away.

I remember the tension. I can almost still feel it now. We could never get Tyler back, so this trial was not going to provide joy or fulfilment. At best, it was going to provide justice for Mark's terrible act, but that was, in a way, seeking revenge. Nevertheless, that's what our whole family expected and craved. Our son was murdered, and the killer had to pay.

But the defense wanted to exonerate Mark, that was their job and the fervent hope of his family. They were nice people. I had met them at Tyler's celebration of life and had passing, ever-brief conversations with Mark's mother, sister and step-father in court hallways. Of course, they wanted to fight for their son. Who could blame them?

Their attorney did his very best to have Mark found innocent. He was good at his job, and I couldn't help but respect him for that. He had a strategy that involved a very painstaking presentation of evidence, but it was likely the only chance there was to reduce Mark's time in jail or perhaps eliminate jail time altogether. He needed to instill the possibility of doubt in at least one juror's mind. Was it less than certain that Mark had shot Tyler?

I studied journalism in college and had some brief experience later as a news person. I was trained to look at things objectively. Whether majoring in journalism and working on the college newspaper molded me or I gravitated toward journalism because I had those instincts, I don't know. Whatever the cause and against my wishes, I looked at Mark's case through that objective lens.

Even with this trial that involved so much emotion, I did find everything about the proceedings to be fascinating. For one thing, the setting. The nice but small and rather dated, drab, wood-themed courtroom was certainly not a big city courtroom with high ceilings, major scale and magnificent trimmings.

The judge, decked out in his traditional black gown that resembled a priest, made his solemn entrance and earned instant respect as the courtroom went suddenly silent every day. The defendant was a focal point of attention, and it was hard not to stare. Mark mostly looked down, somber and sad, which was likely coached. The onlookers, some supporting our family, some supporting Mark's, some just fascinated by a big case in their small town, were seated next to and behind us and usually filled the courtroom.

The proceedings were, naturally, completely two-sided. The district attorney argued fervently for the weight of all the evidence he laid out, while the defense countered, contending there just was no proof that this was a murder. That was the chief point of his case. Naturally, I was emotionally involved with our side. I felt disloyal for any secret lapses of objectivity when I felt my heart and head should have been absolutely committed to our side of the battle.

I did fight, though. I assumed that the more media coverage this trial could receive, the bigger the deal it would be in the town of San Luis Obispo and the more pressure it would exert on the jury to reach the guilty decision we craved. Even though the jury was instructed not to read or pay attention to media coverage, I felt it would seep in and impress them with the seriousness of the case. If it is a huge case with lots of evidence, wouldn't they pay maximum attention, and wouldn't the defendant likely be guilty?

I thought about the case all the time and wrote memos to the DA and other notes to the key reporters on the case to bring out aspects of the events that might get overlooked. I conducted the media interviews for our side since Terryle – who was the logical person to be quoted – was such a wreck that she couldn't do it. I knew how the media worked and knew how to emphasize a few key points, keep it simple, and not allow myself to be sidetracked. I knew to be succinct. If you talk long, things come out wrong.

Terryle's health had deteriorated to the point that she could not sit in a chair. It caused unbearable pain in her back. She would take a cushion to court every day and kneel in front of her upraised seat, peeking over the seat in front of her. Her back still hurt, but it was at least bearable in this position. I'm sure that onlookers were quite baffled. Some asked us if it was a religious requirement.

Back to our slim grip on sanity at home...

After a month or so, I moved the go-get-the-ball game outside, first with the wiffle golf ball and then with a tennis ball. George was bigger and faster and had played ball before, so he would race off and fetch the ball two or three times before his attention wavered. Gracie would run, too, but he could beat her to the ball. However, once George lost interest, Gracie would take over and keep getting the ball and bringing it back until your arm dropped off. She always found it. George would drift off, go somewhere in the shade and lie down, but Gracie never lost focus or got bored. And she slowly got bigger, faster and more experienced.

Soon enough, she was hustling enough to beat George to the ball. He didn't try his hardest, but she sure did. When she beat him every time for a few days in a row, he stopped trying. She was the undisputed champ at seven or eight months old.

Finally, Tunes and I figured that Gracie was big enough to go on the scooter run, and she followed George and me everywhere I rode, even though her legs were still very short. For the rest of her life, she got a near-daily scooter run.

I was so fortunate to have my two dogs. They kept me going. As it turned out, I had no mental capacity to work or write for those three years. A good chunk of that time was spent in court or with the district attorney, but when there were lulls between trials, I was not productive. A friend gave me a commissioned sales project, but the effort I put in was quite sub-par. I would go into my office, smoke cigarettes, play solitaire and try to make a couple of phone calls.

George and Gracie saved me, plain and simple.

Cross-examination, of course, was pure distress for us to sit through. It seemed that logical points were being contradicted and distorted. The defendant's parents, being very successful, had hired a highly skilled defense attorney, and he did his job.

His strategy was to dispute everything. For example, the DA produced two separate, highly credentialed gun experts who testified that the angle of the gunshot proved that a second person shot Tyler. It would have been impossible for Tyler to shoot himself that way (the bullet angled downward from just above his ear, meaning the gun was above his head when it fired).

The defense produced three expert witnesses who explained how it could have been possible, though not easy, for Tyler to have accidentally fired the deadly shot and killed himself. The testimony was so elaborate, with diagrams and everything, that it took three full days to complete. I could see that the jury's eyes were glazing over with all the repetition and excruciating detail.

The thing the defense fought especially hard against was the presentation of evidence. They would dispute almost everything that was introduced relative to Mark's cover-up after the killing, which meant the jury had to file out again and again while the evidence was presented, and the judge had to rule on allowing it to be officially presented.

What really damaged the prosecution's case was that the judge disallowed almost all of the facts concerning what Mark did after the shooting to be heard by the jury or considered in the verdict. He ruled that all the blatant things Mark did to cover up the shooting – the rug cleaning, the lies to friends, the long delay in reporting the shooting, the ditching Tyler's car – came after the fact and were thus irrelevant to the shooting itself.

The key question in the defense case was whether – beyond any shadow of a doubt – there was proof that Mark shot Tyler, or could Tyler have accidentally pulled the trigger himself?

We heard all the elaborate police investigators' testimony on Mark's actions to cover up the shooting in private segments – with the jury ordered to file out of the courtroom into a waiting room. The judge would then rule, but he decided again and again that the things Mark did after the shooting were not relevant to the shooting itself and could not be heard by the jury. They were screened from facts that we considered to be hugely relevant. The jury didn't know a tenth of what we and all the onlookers knew.

Likewise, the testimony of half a dozen mutual friends was conducted with the jury ordered out. These young people revealed without exception that Mark was a frequent cocaine user (Tyler's post-mortem drug test showed that he had not used any drugs), an out-of-control drinker and had displayed and shot his gun unsafely and irresponsibly several times in places where it was illegal to shoot guns.

Friends thought Mark was reckless and dangerous, particularly when drinking or on drugs, but this testimony was excluded from the jury. They testified that Mark owed Tyler thousands of dollars, and Tyler came to visit because he wanted to be paid. Mark's reluctance to pay was cited as a motive for the killing, but the jury never heard it. Witness after witness made the long trip to San Luis Obispo only to have their testimony discarded. Since Mark had not gone to the police for three days, it was not possible to prove whether he was drunk or high on drugs during the shooting. If he had gunshot residue on his hand, it was too late to find it.

All this testimony was invariably excluded from the official trial with the jury present. The judge ruled that these things were not relevant to Tyler's shooting itself. There were only two witnesses who were actually there...and one was dead. Mark's depiction of what happened was the only eye-witness report.

Tuncs and I, Travis and Tyler's dad testified as well, but we did not have any direct knowledge of that night that translated into evidence. We spoke about Tyler, how much we loved and missed him, how we found out that this was being prosecuted as a murder, what we concluded after hearing all the evidence. How our lives were devastated. I have no doubt that the jury believed us and sympathized, but our testimony did not have much weight as to Mark's guilt.

The one semi-bright spot during this difficult time in our lives was coming home to our dogs. George and Gracie were so glad to see us after being alone all day, and they greeted us with endless affection.

One of the first things I would do when we returned from court was to take the dogs for a scooter ride. If Tunes was having a half-decent day physically, she would come too. We would forget our troubles for a few minutes with the rush of riding up the hill, staying on the narrow trail, dodging rocks, trying to keep up with the dogs, and making it to the sweet view from the top of the hill. The reality was waiting for us back at the bottom, but for now we were somewhere else.

The trial lasted eleven grueling weeks – far longer than anyone had projected. It was the realization of the defense's strategy to obfuscate prosecution facts with endless alternative testimony. The case was far from straightforward, and the jury was worn out.

The jury filed out just after lunch on a Monday. They did not return.

We waited outside the courtroom nervously all day long, sitting or pacing, and then the next day and the next as well, all with no result.

And then they filed back in. The foreman handed his slip of paper to the judge, who read it, and then handed it back. The jury foreman rose to announce the verdict.

"Has the jury reached a decision?" the judge asked

"Yes, your honor,' the foreman said in a somber voice. "We find the defendant not guilty."

We never knew who or how many jury members voted to acquit. It only took one.

You can only imagine how the acquittal shocked and devastated us all the more.

Fortunately, our attorney, Dave Turpin, had filed a wrongful death lawsuit by its deadline, just in case the criminal verdict did not convict. We waited nine more months for that trial to get underway. Nine more months of purgatory. During the process, Turpin found an extremely sharp local attorney – Chris Helenius – to take our side (we were the plaintiffs).

The insurance company that insured Mark's family's properties (his parents owned several, including the home where Tyler was shot) hired the same defense attorney who had done such a competent job defending Mark in the murder trial. But in a wrongful death lawsuit, a great deal of information and testimony can be introduced to the jury that is excluded in a criminal trial. This jury heard everything this time.

After a few more painful weeks of trial, the jury returned after one day of deliberation to vote in favor of our side and grant a healthy award. As gratifying as the result was, the greater joy was the entire jury walking up to us after the verdict, one-by-one, to greet us and, hug us and express their sympathy. Several shared tears with us. This jury had ruled unanimously in our favor. Each person expressed his or her condolences and disbelief that the criminal trial verdict was not guilty.

A few weeks after the second trial, I was wrestling around with our dogs when I clearly realized what a sweet role they had played in preserving our sanity, at least what was left. George and especially the beautiful puppy, Gracie, just by being themselves, produced enough light to keep our world from being totally dark. Just looking at them being themselves broadcast love into my life and always had. The honesty, purity and unreserved love that is a dog's nature enriches a human's life. It is a steadying force of good that wags and licks and nudges a human in a positive direction and I, for one, certainly appreciated it.

George was winding down in his exuberant life, but Gracie was just beginning to deliver one amazing contribution after another to the good things life has to offer.

We had thought about mating Gracie since she was a puppy, so we never had her spayed. (George had been neutered, so he was not a candidate to be a father.) Gracie was 3 ½, which was the perfect age for giving birth, our vet told us.

Great friends of mine in Los Angeles loved Golden Retrievers as much as Terryle and I did, and they owned a healthy young male named Kirby. My friends Bruce and Ria agreed to let their dog try to get Gracie pregnant, with them entitled to the pick of the litter from among the puppies if Gracie delivered.

A couple of months after the wrongful death trial, when Gracie was in heat, I brought her to Los Angeles for the weekend. Terryle wanted to go but was too sick to make the journey. I rang the doorbell and heard loud barking. Moments later, the door opened and lunging forward, barking loud and strong, was Kirby, a very large, handsome, powerful, male Golden Retriever, barely being restrained by my friend. Gracie took one look at him and bolted down the block.

Kirby was huge, weighing well over 100 pounds. He was raring to go, although he couldn't have possibly imagined that this was going to be the greatest weekend of his life. I rounded up Gracie and led her back to my friends' backyard gate.

We entered into the yard, and my friends let Kirby out through a side door of the house. I was nervous; would they become lovers, or would he tear her to shreds? I figured, though, that his being a Golden Retriever, how vicious could he be? After a tense fifteen seconds of sniffing and posturing, L'amour took over and ruled the weekend. Courting and romance were never really in consideration.

Gracie did indeed get pregnant, and our vet told us that she would deliver in roughly sixty-two days. That projected to be the last week of July. But Gracie was days late, and because she had still not given birth to her puppies as July rolled into August, there was a chance that she would deliver on a very special day. We crossed our fingers.

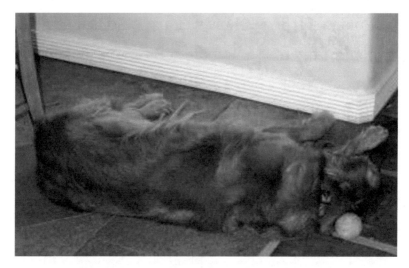

Gracie was never far from her ball, sometimes
holding it until she went to sleep.

Chapter Nine: The Greatest Ball Chaser in the World

It's not the size of the dog in the fight,
it's the size of the fight in the dog.

. -Mark Twain

Gracie Allen, George Burns 1999

It was approaching three years since our son had been killed and just a few months after the conclusion of the wrongful death trial. Terryle and I were trying to adjust to life without Tyler, but it was really hard. I might be trying to do some normal work, but then the thought of Tyler sliding off the chair to the floor, instantly dead or abandoned – crumpled in that dumbwaiter dead and alone – would take over my thoughts, cruelly sinking my stomach and my spirit.

Tunes and I knew that life would go on and the pain would slowly ebb, that "time heals all wounds," but that didn't brighten the dark days. We were still in therapy and inching forward in learning to deal with our loss. The horror of it all was not quite as constant, not quite as sharp a presence in our lives. I thought about Tyler every day, but not every moment of every day. We tried to do normal things and let some light into our lives.

I suspected that it was a little easier for me, but Tunes was Tyler's mother, and that bond was forever. I felt terrible that she was grieving more than me.

Friends and family were a constant source of support. They did a good job of staying in our everyday lives and creating excursions and diversions to reintroduce warmth and some good times. They really tried hard, and it did help.

Best of all, we did not have to go to court anymore. The courtroom experience had been depressing and smothered our lives, but the final outcome of the second trial did finally deliver a glint of positivity for us. It felt a little more like justice had been done.

Court cases are wracked with tension. If you have an emotional connection to either side, the stakes are very high. The fear of losing is paralyzing in any kind of trial.

The attorney who won our wrongful death case, Chris Helenius, did a terrific job. He had come highly recommended and was masterful in how he conducted the trial. Chris won our confidence the day we met him and never let us down. He knew what he needed to accomplish and succeeded in orchestrating a very compelling case.

Chris was not exactly a commanding figure. He was blonde, around 5'9", wide-faced, a little chunky and quite casual in his manner. His suits were nice but not elegant-nice. He was very articulate and could be quite funny in private, but he was all business in the courtroom. Chris developed an excellent rapport with our jury and never failed to effectively present the evidence he wanted. He knew what he desired from witnesses and persisted until he got it. Chris had a folksy way of speaking to the jury that seemed to endear him to them.

After a few tough court sessions of the wrongful death trial, when our confidence was clearly beaten down, Chris made sure to reassure Terryle and me. He would take us aside for pep talks.

"You look worried, but just look at me if your confidence is ever wavering. I mean it, ever. Ask yourself this: Does Chris look worried?

"You never need to be concerned unless I look worried. And that will probably never happen in this case. I like where it's going."

After the closing arguments of the case, as the jury left to deliberate the verdict, I asked him if he thought we would win.

"Of course," he answered. "Do I look worried?"

We were getting a break for lunch every day, which was a relief from the tension of the trial but also a surreal experience since our heads were in such a weird place. Tunes and I would walk around day after day, seeing the sights of the charming downtown district of San Luis Obispo, but the walk was not uplifting. It was like a gray fog obscured everything so that nothing was truly special or truly beautiful. And no matter how tasty the lunch might have been, it was never all that enjoyable for us. Flavors were bland, and we generally did not have much appetite.

We were in a hurry to get back into the courtroom but dreaded going back into the courtroom.

Occasionally we ate lunch with Chris, on the days he didn't have to rush to his office to oversee other business. We would ask questions about the trial, and his answers were both reassuring and interesting. We learned a lot from Chris' analysis of witnesses, strategies and how he expected things to progress.

Beyond that, Chris was a lively conversationalist, and it was nice being able to disengage from the trial at times to just talk about things in general.

One day at lunch, the conversation turned to dogs, and I found myself bragging to Chris about how our three-year-old Golden Retriever, Gracie, was uncanny in her ability to find the ball. She never failed.

"Our dog, Gracie Allen, is the greatest ball fetcher I've ever seen," I announced. "She never fails to bring the ball back, ever. She's uncanny. Gracie will make her way down a mountainside, climb up inside a thick hedge, comb every inch of a hillside thick with rocks and chaparral, swim across a stream – anything it took – but she will always find her ball and bring it back.

"On occasion, it could take an hour or even more. But she will not allow herself to fail. She'll show up eventually with the ball in her mouth. She is relentless."

Midway through my congratulatory speech about Gracie, Chris' lips curved up into the tiniest of smiles. By the end, he was grinning very knowingly. It was a borderline smirk. I saw this and had to stop talking to find out what he was grinning about.

"What?" I asked indignantly.

"Gracie sounds like a real champion," Chris said, "but my dog, Ciervo (which means 'deer' in Spanish), is the greatest ball chaser who ever lived. He gets the ball every time. He's gone against other great ball chasers and creamed them all. He's really fast, really smart, has an incredible nose and a deep determination to win. He never loses. Never even comes close."

Now it was my turn to laugh (although it came out a bit hollow because I was secretly wondering if his dog would actually defeat mine in a contest).

"OK, Chris," I said. "When this trial is over, we need to have a contest. And we'll need to put up a little money. Because Ciervo will never beat Gracie!"

"I can't wait," he replied.

After the jury awarded our side the winning verdict in our wrongful death case, we embraced Chris and our own attorney, Dave Turpin, and expressed our deep thanks for their huge roles in getting us the vindication we needed. We could finally breathe.

That felt surreal, too.

Two or three months after the second trial ended and just before Gracie's exciting, love-filled weekend in Los Angeles, Chris and I were wrapping up some legal issues on the phone when I remembered our challenge. I invited him to lunch at my house.

"Bring your dog and your wallet," I said.

"You're a good guy, Dave," he replied. "It's going to be a shame to humiliate you."

I have to admit it: I didn't expect us to win. I could do bravado with the best of them, but the way Chris described Ciervo, I figured he was a unique talent. Still, I was so appreciative of Chris that I wanted to keep our friendship going. Any chance to get together outside the court environment would be welcome. It would be great to visit with him even if his dog came away as the champion.

And defeating Gracie was not going to be easy.

We met at the cottage Tunes, and I were renting in Solvang, located on a rugged but beautiful cattle ranch and winery. It was owned by a lovely couple: Stevan Larner, a successful long-time cinematographer in Hollywood – he was the principal camera operator for "Murder She Wrote" and numerous other television shows and movies – and his delightfully colorful wife, Christine, who was French. They were very nice to us.

The rental was a unique place, on top of a low hill, surrounded by loads of oak trees and the natural terrain of the Southern California foothills. Tunes and I often threw the ball for Gracie off the front side of the hill, which was overgrown with natural vegetation. We could throw it in any forward direction, and it would fly out of sight, over the edge and down the slope. We wanted to make sure it would be challenging for Gracie to find it because any straight throw would have been a walk in the park. It made it more interesting for everyone.

Gracie couldn't actually see where the ball went as it disappeared down the hill, but she always paid attention to the general location, and we could hear her down below somewhere bulling her way through the sage, scrub oak, woody bushes and cacti of California's natural chaparral to locate the ball. It was tough terrain down there. She would not be able to follow the ball's progress to the ultimate location once it disappeared over the hillside, but would always watch the throw, get a sense of direction and rely on her keen nose to find it every time.

So I knew we had a natural home-field advantage. What I didn't know was that Ciervo and Chris had a particular trick up their sleeve that was going to make them very hard to beat.

Chris brought Ciervo over and he and Gracie sniffed and did their greetings, then jumped and wrestled around a little, obviously getting along well. Ciervo was not quite as tall or long as Gracie, but he looked very muscular. He was a mixed breed, tawny in color, with terrier and retriever characteristics. Ciervo weighed around 50 pounds.

He was high energy – not so much a people dog – but more interested in running around, exploring the yard and schmoozing with Gracie.

"We actually found Ciervo wandering around a small town in Baja, California," Chris told me. "The dog didn't seem to have any owners, or at least he wasn't wearing any kind of collar, and we know there are plenty of street strays down there. We asked several people if they knew who he belonged to, but no one had any answers.

"Anyway, he tagged around with us all day, and my wife Lynn said we ought to try to keep him. I told her that they would confiscate him at the border, but we could try. Amazingly, they waved us right through. I'm not sure they even saw him. Ever since we got home with him, he's been a great dog.

"I saw from the very beginning how fast he was. Fastest I've ever seen. I started throwing him the ball and he got so good it blew my mind. He's a wizard.

"Sorry, but you're going down."

Chris and I had lunch on the patio and continued our mutual razzing.

"Ciervo looks nervous," I observed. "Wow, very nervous. He's worried that this terrain is just too tough for him and might make it impossible for him to find the ball."

"Are you kidding? That's his competition look. He can't wait to get started!"

"I don't know. Ciervo is looking around like he's already lost. Scared out of his mind. I'm liking our chances."

"Hah!" Chris came right back, "Ciervo is looking around to see if there are going to be any tougher dogs than a Golden Retriever that he has to beat today. He's not used to this being so easy. So let's make this interesting," he added. "What do you say we play this for 100 bucks." He opened his wallet and slapped a hundred-dollar bill on the table.

So now I was way less confident.

"Uh, let's make it $20," I suggested in a voice that came out weaker and higher than I intended. He laughed out loud and couldn't get the grin off his face as he sipped his beer, displaying a subtle but irritating bravado. He acted like he had won already.

I'll say it again. I was worried.

We agreed on a best-of-seven World Series format, so the first dog to four retrievals would be the winner. Chris got the first throw and heaved it mightily – well over the hill to our left at an angle of about nine o'clock from where we were standing in front of the patio table. Ciervo took off instantly, at top speed, and left Gracie in the dust. You could tell she was confused because she had never faced any real, "professional" opposition before...and especially not one deploying that run-as-fast-as-you-can technique.

Her bewilderment was obvious by her body language as she trotted after Ciervo, well behind him. Chris was chuckling loud enough for me to hear. No doubt at all that it was for my benefit.

Ciervo was coming back over the hill just about the same time that Gracie was about to descend. She was stunned to see Ciervo trot past her, seeming to show off the ball as he went by. She had been thoroughly beaten. She straggled back, looking depressed. It was 1-0. Things were not looking good.

I made the next throw, hurling the ball roughly as far as Chris had to a slightly different spot further to the right. Ciervo took off again, but this time Gracie ran, too. Not as fast as her male competitor – he was damn fast – but not that far behind. He disappeared over the hill, and so did she a second or two later.

We heard the two dogs tearing through the brush down below with no idea who was going to win this round. Chris was very confident that it would be Ciervo. I was really hopeful but less than confident that it would be Gracie.

After a couple of minutes, both dogs appeared at the top of the hill. I was amazed and thrilled to see that Gracie had the ball. A confused and mortified Ciervo was nipping away, trying to steal it. It was as if it was rightfully his and she had no right to even think it was hers. Anyway, she wasn't giving it up, and she trotted back grandly and proudly to tie it up 1-1.

Was there a glimmer of hope?

Chris threw next and he tried a different direction, heaving it powerfully way over the hill at more like three o'clock. Ciervo, naturally, took off like a jet, cranking those legs faster than ever toward the crest of the hill. Gracie was running fast, too, but a few steps behind. They disappeared down the hill and we heard the usual rough rustling in the brush as they scrounged around looking for the ball. After a short while, Gracie came back into sight. She had the ball!

Ciervo was taking a while coming back up. Maybe he didn't see that Gracie had the ball already. Chris had to call him, and when he came up to us and saw Gracie with the ball in her mouth, he seemed confused.

The good guys were ahead, though, 2-1. I was starting to feel just a little giddy, but it was not over.

I threw it straight ahead, and the dogs took off. Ciervo was so damn fast that he, of course, led all the way, those little legs churning into a blur. Gracie ran her usual way at more like a fast lope. Ciervo could certainly outrun her, and I was glad that was not what we were betting on.

The dogs were gone a long time on this round. Of course, we couldn't see down the hill from where we were standing, but after waiting, Chris asked, "Shall we go look at what's happening down there?"

"Sure, good idea," I said.

We jogged the fifty feet or so to the edge of the downslope and spotted the dogs churning their way through the tall underbrush. It was really thick there. At times, the dogs almost disappeared in the density of the growth. Gracie had a technique of starting in one area and then branching out into wider and wider circles until she found a ball. Ciervo seemed to be doing something similar, but his search was a bit more random. Their techniques were impeded, though, by the thickness of the chaparral.

We weren't sure where the ball had landed, and obviously, the dogs weren't either. It almost never took this long, and I wondered what the problem could be. After all, they both had great noses.

Finally, Gracie dived under a thick, brambly bush and emerged with the ball along with a mouthful of debris. Instead of coming straight back up the hill, she waltzed over to a small clearing near where Ciervo was searching and flaunted her prize. She stood there, almost posing, to make sure he saw that she had it. Once he figured out that she had won again, his tail drooped. He seemed depressed. I actually felt bad for him, but not all that bad, and I did have a big smile on my face.

We walked back to the picnic bench in silence. Gracie was now ahead 3-1 and had won three straight. Our team had the momentum, and I did not think the mighty Gracie was going to be beaten. We made it back to our throwing spot, and Chris said begrudgingly, half under his breath, "that Gracie is damn good. We could lose this thing."

He threw it way off to the left this time, about where he heaved it the first time, and we were shocked to see something very different happen. Gracie took off at her full speed but then slowed a bit – still faster than she would normally run if we were just playing alone – but below her top speed. She kept looking back.

But Ciervo did not move. Didn't budge one inch. He had stopped caring about the contest or acted that way, anyway. He wouldn't look in the direction of the ball, either. For that matter, he wouldn't look at us. He just laid down, conceding. Chris shook his head, not quite in disgust, more like in acceptance. Gracie took her sweet time, located the ball and came back the winner. She wanted to play some more.

Chris was very gentlemanly about it and freely admitted that our dog was the champion. We had another beer or two and got laughing again, our friendship warm and strong. Gracie laid down next to Ciervo, rolled him the ball, and before too long they were friends again.

As we got up for him to leave, something came over me, and I just had to say it. The words popped into my head and came out of my mouth before I could stop them. I swear, I never planned it, never even thought of it until that moment. It was inadvertent. I shouldn't have said those words, though. I should have been better than that. I wasn't some 12-year-old smart-ass. I should have shown some restraint, some maturity...some grace and sportsmanship, for God's sake.

But I did say it.

"Are you worried yet?"

Petey came later, but he was the only one of our dogs who could have rivaled Gracie in ball chasing. She would have won, though.

Chapter Ten: Puppies

Whoever said you can't buy happiness

forgot about little puppies

-   Gene Hill

Gracie and the puppies 1999

Tunes and I had never raised puppies, so when Gracie got pregnant, we read books on the subject and talked to friends who had gone through the experience to learn what to expect. There was a lot of information to digest, and we were definitely on pins and needles as the time of birth drew nearer, but we figured we were now as ready as we could be.

We were just assuming that Gracie was, too.

The instructions advised that we prepare a "birthing box" with raised sides so Gracie could keep her puppies together and nurse them...and they could more easily huddle together for warmth and companionship. The idea was that the puppies

168

could not get out of their birthing box until they were three or four weeks old and big and strong enough to climb over the wall of the box.

I built a very simple bed out of plywood that was six feet by four feet with one-foot-high sides. We moved some furniture around and designated our guest room downstairs as the puppy room.

We also put a lamp next to the birthing box and fitted it with an infrared bulb to keep the puppies warm in the early stages of their lives. They wouldn't have hair at first or very much real ability to generate body heat, so they could go into shock and die on a cold night. The books said they would huddle together to keep each other warm and cuddle up with their mother to share her body warmth, but it still advised an infrared light.

We took Gracie to our local veterinarian twice. The first time was when we suspected that she was pregnant. It had been about three weeks since our attempt to breed her, so we wanted to find out if it worked. Gracie was not fat but seemed maybe a little pudgy, with the extra weight showing in her stomach, especially the lower part. Our vet confirmed that Gracie was pregnant and gave us the timeline (the gestation time for all dog breeds is roughly nine weeks) on when we should expect her to give birth.

The second time was when Gracie was about two weeks out. She still was not super heavy, not like a human mother, but was definitely showing. Our vet predicted the day but said it could vary by a few days either way.

"Can you tell how many puppies she's going to have?" Tunes asked.

"I can't tell you precisely," the vet replied, "but it's going to be several."

"Good!" we both said simultaneously, then smiled at each other.

Energy-wise, Gracie had slowed down just a bit, but she was still obsessed with chasing the ball. We've had dogs who loved ball playing however Gracie took it to an otherworldly plateau of ball obsession. (She was the greatest ball chaser in the world, after all.) So, she still chased the ball, but we took it really easy on her and forced her to stop after two or three throws. By no means did Gracie want to quit, but we didn't want her to push it. Meanwhile, my arm thanked me for the decision.

The vet had told us that we could expect her to give birth in ten days or so or any time after. He gave us a book to read that had good information, and we had read a couple of other books with essentially the same guidance.

Tunes and I were as ready as we could be for this unprecedented adventure, but Gracie was late. A couple of days passed beyond the vet's projection, and still no babies. Suddenly it seemed possible that the puppies might be born on August 3, Tyler's birthday. It was still a long shot, but it certainly would have made for a slightly nicer epilogue to the most horrible chapter in our lives.

The days went by until one day before Tyler's birthday. We had shifted from daily scooter rides to walking with Gracie up the same scenic hill behind our house. Tunes was walking her that day, and when she returned, she told me she thought Gracie was ready. She had stopped on her walk after 100 feet or so and wouldn't go on. She was breathing rather heavily, too.

"Wow, I'm so excited!" Tunes gushed.

"Me too!" I agreed. "A little nervous, but incredibly excited."

"It should be interesting," she said.

We took Gracie into the "puppy room" and lifted her onto a beach towel on the bed with

Tunes. It was now early evening, and Gracie was in somewhat of a mental zone, mostly impervious to anything we did, preparing her body to give birth. She didn't want to eat or drink water. We both wanted to be there with Gracie, but we made sure at least one of us was always there if the other had to run out for a minute.

We were hoping that Gracie could hold out for just this one more night and give birth on Tyler's birthday.

We were on the bed, trying to stay awake, and Gracie was lying next to Tunes. Our plan was to have Tunes gently provide any help to Gracie in pulling babies out and cleaning the placenta and birth remnants off each puppy. Then, she would place the puppy on Gracie's stomach at a nipple. Although the puppies would be too young to nurse, the vet said doing this got them comfortable with being on her belly and finding the nipple.

Next, Tunes was going to hand the puppy to me. I would lift up my shirt and hold the puppy to my bare stomach for a couple of minutes to warm it up and perhaps provide a little security through body-to-body contact. Ultimately, I would gently put the newborn puppy in the dog bed under the infrared light.

We had no idea how many puppies Gracie would have. Five? Eight? We hoped for at least a few.

I dozed off, but Tunes did her best to stay awake in order to help Gracie. At some point, she helped Gracie slide off the bed and curl up alone on the floor. Tunes shook me at midnight.

"It's a new day, babe," she said. "Gracie is going to have her babies on Tyler's birthday."

"That is awesome," I said. "Somebody is intervening here, big time. Happy birthday, Tyler."

"Happy birthday!"

We "clinked" imaginary glasses and celebrated Tyler's birthday plus the impending births as best we could, being dead tired. Later that day, we opened a bottle of champagne.

It was just after 2 a.m. when Gracie started making quiet sounds of distress. She was giving birth to puppy number one! Gracie had no trouble squeezing the placenta sac out and started to eat it. Mother dogs do this instinctively to hide the smells and remnants of birth from predators.

After Gracie licked her puppy clean, she immediately began to show signs that another was coming. Tunes gently lifted the tiny, wet, shivering firstborn and gently wiped it off further with a towel.

"Hi, little angel," she said in a sweet voice. "We're so happy to welcome you to our family. Your mommy just gave birth to you one minute ago. See, here she is right here. Now you're going to have a wonderful life. You are so beautiful. We love you so, so much.

"And Gracie, you did such a great job. Your puppy is so beautiful! You are going to be the BEST mommy."

Then she placed the puppy onto Gracie's chest, held it against Gracie's nipple for perhaps thirty seconds, then handed the puppy to me. I cuddled it for a few minutes and then gently laid the puppy in the dog box directly under the glow of the heat lamp.

It was an amazing experience for me to hold this little living thing. It was so tiny – about the size of my fist. It wiggled and squirmed just a bit every few seconds. I tried to gently determine the puppy's sex but just couldn't. I marveled at the beauty and simplicity of our dog giving birth.

"Hi, li'l sweetheart," I half-whispered. "You're the prettiest puppy ever. You're going to grow up to be a Golden Retriever and have so much fun in your life." I had the biggest smile on my face. It stayed there for a long time.

Gracie gave birth to her second puppy, and we had a slight lull. So she had time to lick and chew the sac. Gracie ate pretty much all of it, however, the vet had cautioned us that the placenta sac was not going to agree with her, and she would likely throw it up, especially if there were a lot of puppies. So Tunes had the basic strategy of taking it away from Gracie if she possibly could.

"Hi, sweetheart," she said softly. "We love you so much!"

Tunes handed puppy number two to me. I cuddled it, talked to it soothingly and then placed it right next to its sibling. I made sure they were touching so they would get a little warmth and comfort from each other, but they were doing that instinctively anyway. They were squirming around like crazy. Their eyes were closed.

Man, they were tiny!

Most of the puppies came at short intervals. Tunes alternated between narrating the action to me and talking to Gracie comfortingly. She would coax Gracie on and compliment her on doing such a great job. Tunes welcomed each puppy in the same loving voice.

Tunes talking to the puppies was adorable. I leaned over and gave her a kiss.

Gracie gave birth to eight puppies in not quite three hours. Then she stopped. We figured that she was finished and rejoiced that we had eight beautiful new puppies...all born on Tyler's birthday. As we thought back about this over the next few weeks and months, it seemed like our puppies were a special gift of love directly from our son.

I placed them so they were all touching, but a couple rolled away from the group where they were squirming, isolated and alone. I kept my eyes open and moved any rovers back into the main grouping. One puppy was noticeably smaller than the rest. I didn't know what to think of that.

Tunes got her first chance to stand up, stretch her legs, and walk over to view the group of eight puppies inside the puppy box. They were too young to be cute, exactly – still pink and hairless, skin a bit blotchy, eyes closed – but still a marvel to behold. There were constant, squealy "eeps" coming from various puppies that never stopped.

Gracie got up to walk around a bit but did not go to the puppy box. Instead, she went to the door; however, we didn't want to let her out of the room. We had brought in a water bowl and a food bowl, and Gracie took a few slurps of water.

I called our friend Carmen, who lived nearby and had been very supportive as Gracie's time got close. I assumed that she would be sleeping, so I left a single word as the message: "Ocho." Carmen was of Hispanic heritage, and I knew she'd figure out what that short message referred to and get a kick out of it.

She did, but there were more surprises in store for all of us.

After around a 45-minute lull, Gracie went back into labor. She didn't really signal anything...she just pumped out another puppy sac. We were amazed and didn't know what else to expect. Fifteen minutes later, Gracie did it again. When she finally stopped, the total was up to twelve tiny Golden Retriever puppies, six boys and six girls.

Gracie drank some water, and we let her out to go to the bathroom, but she came right back, climbed into the birthing box and laid down with her puppies. She attempted to cuddle the pile without squishing anybody, and the puppies squirmed around to get next to their mom or at least cuddle other puppies who were touching. Coordination was not easy with so many. One had rolled away by a few feet and was whining constantly. ("Eeping is really a better word because it sounded like "Eep, eep, eep.") We placed it back next to Gracie.

The puppies were a sea of motion, wiggling and squirming all over each other in a constantly changing puppy pile around their mom. No doubt that a few were asleep at various times, but whichever puppies were awake agitated around enough to make up for any deficit.

Tunes and I slept in the puppy room however we were so excited that we didn't sleep much. One of us got up periodically to make sure no puppies were alone and cold. Somebody often was, so we moved it back to the pile. The eeping never stopped, no matter what.

Sometime after dawn, we got up and began a stretch of days that were full of wonder but also seemed to last an eternity with too little sleep and so much to do. Who knew?

We had arranged to have our vet come to the house on the day.

Gracie gave birth to check the new mother and examine all the puppies. He came over after his regular workday and gave us a good report. That was when we learned we had six girls and six boys. (Our vet did caution us about the little runt of the litter needing help to survive.)

"Your puppies and their mama look good so far," he told us. "You want to place them on Gracie's nipples tomorrow morning so they can learn to nurse. You'll get the knack of it, and so will they. Let's have you bring them into my office in a week so we can weigh them and examine them again. Call me if you have any concerns."

We had learned from our books to line the puppy box with fresh newspaper once or twice every day to gather their puppy poop (and pee), so it could be disposed of while we put down fresh newspaper. I had stored loads of newspaper for this purpose. We had a last-minute idea to ensure greater warmth and comfort, though, so we covered the floor of the puppy box with a layer of beach towels and laid a couple of blankets on top.

That might have been comfy, but the beddings did not make it very long before they had to be washed. After changing the beddings four or five times per day for a couple of days and running the washing machine non-stop, we pivoted back to the newspaper concept.

The books said we might be surprised by the volume of puppy poop...but that was a pitiful understatement. Surprised? In no way did we anticipate the enormous loads they actually managed to crank out. How could they each poop more than their body weight several times a day? Because that was, I'm pretty sure, the reality of it.

Tunes or I had to change newspapers at least four times a day and clean up the puppies endlessly because they had no problem cheerfully stepping, sleeping and rolling in poop or anything else that was under them. We knew raising puppies would be a lot of work, but we could have spent twenty-four hours a day on the poop/clean-up aspect alone.

We had a fundamental problem in that Gracie only had ten nipples in two rows that matched up, but there were twelve hungry puppies to feed. To make matters worse, only eight nipples were yielding milk. So right there, we had to devise a way the puppies could feed in shifts.

We named the runt of the litter "Gidget," which in surfing lore stood for "girl midget." She was the only puppy with a name for a few weeks. Little Gidget was just two-thirds the size of her siblings and when scrambling to the nipple, she was easily pulled back and kicked to the bottom by flailing paws. It wasn't intentional on the part of the other puppies but just happened in the mad scrum.

(In fact, the vet told us that it was statistically unlikely that all twelve puppies would survive and that the runt was most likely to get progressively weaker in competition with her bigger, stronger sisters and brothers.)

So we took special measures to ensure that Gidget could nurse, putting her on a nipple first before we let any of the others get a chance to feed. Then we would slowly add more puppies but made sure that Gidget could get her fill. It worked. Gidget never grew to be as large as the others, but she did survive and had a nice, active life with my brother Glenn's family. They always talked about what a sweet dog she was.

Watching the puppies nurse in those first few days was an amazing scene. Their eyes were still closed, so they did it all by pure instinct. They would flail their little arms and legs, climbing and squirming until they found a nipple, then suck like crazy for their sustenance. They were loud, too, slurping away like there was no such thing as respectable puppy etiquette. In fact, let's call a spade a spade; they were downright greedy.

Individual puppies would often slip off and then get paddled downward by the constant "swimming" motion of the pups on either side. They would frantically crawl back up Gracie's stomach to an open nipple and get slurping again. Puppies were shifting nipples all over the place. Knocked off one, find another. Need to paw somebody out of the way? Don't give it a second thought.

When a puppy was satiated, it pushed off and was promptly paddled out of the milk zone by the ever-pumping arms and legs of more eager siblings. When it didn't try to crawl back, we took it out of the action zone until feeding was over.

A significant complication was that Gracie did not like nursing her puppies. She was less than ambivalent about that little responsibility. The literature says a mother dog has strong motherly instincts and will nurse her dogs until they are roughly four weeks old, at which time they start to get their teeth and begin to introduce pain into the equation.

But Gracie's willingness to nurse lasted only a little over two weeks. Maybe it was the chaos of all those puppies clamoring to get milk at once with their overwhelming twelve-to-one ratio. Or perhaps it was the way they sucked and pawed at her so aggressively.

I figured she just wanted to get back to her real priority – playing ball.

Whatever the reason, after two weeks or so, Gracie did not want to go back into the puppy box. She had to be carried. (She weighed nearly seventy pounds and did not cooperate, so that was quite a challenge. No need to tell you who the designated carrier was.) That worked for a few days, but after that, I would lay her down inside the dog bed, and she would get right up and leave.

Soon, the puppies were climbing out of the wood box – a hilarious sight – and they would scramble after their mother like crazy little vampires as she walked back and forth across the room, trying her best to make sure nobody ever caught up.

On a very rare occasion, Gracie would stop and allow her puppies to nurse as long as they could rise up, stand on two feet and hold onto a nipple. It was an amazing sight, but we didn't see it much. And that was pretty much the end of Gracie's motherly instincts.

The vet helped us devise a food concoction for the puppies to substitute for mother's milk that consisted of blending a high-vitamin puppy chow and a special, nutritious dry milk, plus enough water to make it a liquid. Then we'd run it in the blender for a minute or so.

At first, we would fill up a little bowl and hold it under one squirming puppy at a time while it licked up its fill of nutrition. We had to wear a towel because far more liquid food splashed out than went into a puppy. Likewise, there was way more food on the puppy's face than in his/her tummy. And don't even get me started on the front paws that just had to splash around in the emulsion before the face could dip in.

We soon came up with the plan to use aluminum foil paint roller trays, which are elevated at the top so that the paint (or liquid puppy food) flows to the wider bottom. Then, we lined up four puppies, one at each tray, to take their sustenance. It took a while for them to figure it out, but after a little time, the first one started to slurp up his/her dinner, and soon the others joined in, too. Gidget was always in on the first shift along with three others, and then we replaced them with four new customers.

I say "dinner," but these guys had to eat at least five or six times a day. It's hard to say which one was dinner.

One more slight complication to this scenario: the puppies did not stand there and eat from their respective tray in a polite and orderly manner. They did not have or care about any manners whatsoever. Oh no. They stepped in, tromped around, got food all over their wicked little bodies, romped over to the next guy's tray, climbed all through that one, too, rotated down the line, made an amazing mess on the sides of the trays, the floor around them, the wall (how they got the wall astounds me to this day), and, of course, themselves.

(It only took one feeding to realize we needed to line the floor under the food trays with plenty of newspaper, too.)

So, we had to take each one into another room, rinse them off, dry them and put them back into the doggy box while we introduced the next shift to repeat the process. We had to prepare several batches of food for each feeding. By the time we finished feeding all twelve little varmints, and after cleaning them up along with the floor and walls and washing out each tray, it was time to make more food and get ready to do it again.

In light of the constant prep work, Tunes and I stopped laughing about how cute and ridiculous this was after a day or two. We were so tired! We got to the point where we loved our puppies and would do anything for them, but, as for ourselves, personally, pretty much didn't care if we ate, showered or kept the house tidy. We just wanted to sleep.

What saved us was our friend Sue coming down from Northern California for a week with her young daughter Natalie and her best friend, Lauren. The ten-year-old girls loved helping with all of this. They thought it was the cutest thing in the world. We even progressed to the point of marching the herd out into the backyard, where they could frolic in the grass, wrestle with each other, and, of course, go to the bathroom.

We always laughed, watching these pudgy little guys waddle through the house in joyous efforts to get to the open sliding door to the backyard. They loved it outside and ultimately would not come back into the house of their own volition. They had zero interest in the return phase. So, we had to carry them. We'd put them back in their puppy box, but they would instantly jump right back out. We had to close the door, or they would magically show up outside again like they never left.

The puppies were entering the cute stage by now, where they progressed from looking like newborn little ragamuffins into plump, fluffy Golden Retriever puppies. Most adorable things in the world.

But they were still so small that any number of animals could have snatched one. We put up a wire fence around a good portion of the yard, mostly under a big oak tree, so hawks or eagles couldn't swoop down in a surprise attack. We'd leave them out there for an hour or so – with at least one supervising person always inside the fence with them.

As puppies do, they would run, jump on a buddy, wrestle whoever was close, bite, chew and play, play, play until they dropped in their tracks, instantly asleep. They could sleep any time, any place. By the way, being asleep didn't stop any other random puppy from chewing on them, stepping on their head, pouncing on top or pulling them around by the tail, but they were gone to the world for a while and didn't care.

My favorite thing to do was come into the puppy room and get down on my knees. I'd say, "Hi, you guys!" Most of them would be goofing around in their box, but a few were always just poking around the room. Wherever they were, they would all come racing over to me, little fluff balls with tails wagging furiously, then jump up in my lap and leap up to kiss my face. I'd scoop up as many as I could in my arms to keep them from sliding back down, and they would lick furiously. The ones who missed the scoop would climb up the backs of the others and come over the top for me. It was a love frenzy. I would be filled with affection and laughing non-stop at the craziness and wonderfulness of it all. I'd do this four or five times every single day, and the experience was sublime. I have never forgotten it to this day.

The entire experience of having these puppies was exhausting, but it was a pure joy for Tunes and me. Our lives were beautifully enriched by the innocence and exuberance of Gracie's children. They brought a magical element of simple pleasure into our lives when we never thought we'd experience happiness again.

Gracie soon tired of nursing. After a while, she would only nurse for as long as the puppies could stand up and reach for it. What she really wanted to do was play ball. Note the ball just waiting off to her right - Photo courtesy of Janet Thompson.

Gracie nurses her puppies shortly after giving birth

We moved to Ojai when the puppies were six months old and here is Yosemite discovering the creek below our house

Chapter Eleven: Breaking Up the Gang

Better than all of the gold in the world,

Better than diamonds, better than pearls,

Better than any material thing...

Is the love of a dog and the joy it brings.

-Laura Jaworski

Gracie and the puppies, 1999

Our time of puppy bliss was coming to an end, and we knew the inevitable next step was to find loving homes for our babies. We hated the thought that our days of sweet chaos would be over soon and that our beloved puppies' time of perfect happiness with their brothers and sisters was never meant to last forever. We had to break up the gang, but how could we? The only consoling thought was that these chubby little angels would bring joy to many new families, and they would always be loved.

For Tunes and me, this whole adventure was a time we would never forget.

We decided to keep a boy and a girl, in addition to Gracie, and find homes for the ten others. Our friends who supplied the father were getting the pick of the litter. But we were afraid that nine was still a high number and we might not find enough takers.

We spread the word to relatives first. Two of my brothers and a cousin immediately let us know they wanted a puppy, leaving six to go. As it turned out, finding homes wasn't a problem at all. Golden Retriever puppies were in high demand, it seemed, and we could have found homes for twice as many.

Solvang is just a small town, so we placed an ad in the Santa Barbara Independent for Golden Retriever Puppies and priced them at $450 each. The going rate for Goldies was more like $500 each, so we figured that we would have an edge at $450. We offered to let people meet the puppies that upcoming Saturday and Sunday and asked people to call. We got lots of calls.

"I want to keep them all," Tunes announced.

"I know," I said, "but we can't keep twelve dogs. Thirteen, actually, with Gracie. Can you imagine?"

"But I love every one of them. They're beautiful, and so, so sweet. Look at them! How can we possibly choose which two to keep and which ones have to leave?"

"We have to make sure we find great people and great homes for our puppies, then at least we'll know they're in for a good life."

"I know. But choosing is impossible, and I want them all."

Tunes was not wrong. Looking at them hustling around, creating chaos, wherever they went, tan-colored fluff balls with sweet, happy faces, tails always wagging, having so much fun, mischievous in an innocent way...there's no way I could imagine a prettier group of living creatures. I loved each and every one.

"We're in deep trouble," I signed. "I feel the same way exactly."

We both knew, though, that ten puppies had to go.

We were in frequent communication with our friends who supplied the father of the litter. They came up to visit when the puppies were just a few days old and were very excited to hear our reports of the puppies' progress. We invited them to visit a week before we placed the ads in order to select their "pick of the litter." They chose a large, robust, affectionate boy who was just a bit darker than his siblings, and they played with him for over an hour. They could hardly bear to leave.

Our friends named their new puppy "Kane," which was a reference to legendary comic book illustrator Gil Kane (they were huge enthusiasts). The puppies' father, Kirby, was also named after a comic book artist, Jack Kirby.

Then Tunes and I had the difficult task of choosing which boy and girl to select as our own. That was so hard! In fact, it was nearly impossible because of our love and affection for every single one of the puppies. We didn't make our selection until the deadline pressure of the morning the prospective families were coming.

"O.K., we've procrastinated down to the wire," I reminded Tunes.

We have to pick our two puppies, or we'll be stuck taking the last two after the families choose."

"I can't do it," Tunes proclaimed. "There's no way. I can't choose. You'll have to choose."

"Are you serious? I'm not choosing. This has to be a team effort."

After commiserating for a few minutes, we got to it. And once we selected our two, we couldn't help but second guess our choices, thinking that we made a big mistake and should have taken others.

We agreed that we would have to agree on both puppies, but that was not easy at all. I liked a big boy (with big paws indicating he would grow up to be large). He was a noisy boy, making frequent sounds somewhere between humming and whining. We nicknamed him "Whiner." Tunes was worried that he would drive us crazy. I said he was bound to stop being such a baby. He was very handsome and one of the most active puppies.

I lifted him and handed him to Tunes.

"He's beautiful," she love-sighed, pressing her nose against him and smothering him with dozens of kisses. She handed him to me.

I bounced him in my arms and gave a close look at his beautiful face. He immediately lunged forward to give me kisses.

"I think this guy will be a wonderful dog," I said.

With deadline pressure putting the squeeze on, we went with Whiner. He grew into a large, gorgeous Golden Retriever – not the smartest dog in the world, but powerful, affectionate, athletic and good-natured. We named him George Burns II in honor of his classic predecessor, who had died just a year ago. His mom was Gracie Allen, so it seemed automatic.

Choosing the girl was really tough because they were all sweethearts. We debated back and forth, worried that we would somehow let a gem slip away. We didn't choose her until the very last minute before the families were arriving to choose their puppies. We already knew we would name her Yosemite after our favorite place in the world.

We narrowed it down to two possibilities. One was the most affectionate of all the puppies and had a cute but slightly funny face. The other seemed smart and was something of a leader. A gut feeling caused Tunes to pick the affectionate one. Time would tell how good the choice was.

Our vet warned us that parvovirus was a dangerous disease that spread easily and could kill a young puppy. There were a couple of other diseases, too, to be avoided. Even though the puppies had their initial vaccinations, they were still vulnerable to parvo and other diseases, so we had to take protective measures. These diseases could be picked up in a dog park or public places and could be carried around on the bottom of someone's shoes. If a puppy acquired one of these viruses, sickness and possible death were sure to follow.

So, the vet suggested that we spray every visitor's shoe bottoms with a mixture of bleach and water before they had any contact with the puppies. We did this at our front door, and all the prospective families were happy to do it, knowing that just inside the house was going to be a glorious assembly of little darlings.

It was really hard, in fact, impossible, to tell which puppy was which. They were all about the same size and really adorable. So Tunes had painted their toenails with different color combinations and we kept a chart to distinguish who was who.

Most everyone who came to see the puppies was very nice – friendly, enthusiastic, appreciative – and obviously all were dog lovers. Most of them were couples, and the ones who had children brought them, too. My two brothers who wanted puppies were there for the big day, as were my cousins.

It was a relief when my brother Glenn and his wife Kacy insisted on taking home the runt of the litter. They are long-time dog-lovers, and we knew they'd give Gidget a good home. (We were slightly miffed when they renamed her Zoe as if we hadn't hit on the absolute perfect name.)

Every visitor practically swooned when they saw the array of gorgeous puppies. The children screamed with delight. And the puppies were thrilled to have visitors, racing around in total joy, showering our guests with affection. It was excitement multiplied by chaos. But after the initial melee, everyone located and squared off with the puppy they could not wait to take home.

Our visitors were so enthusiastic that, for the most part, the first to arrive were the ones who got puppies. We had plenty of takers by the early afternoon Saturday and told people who came later in the afternoon or called for the Sunday showing that the puppies were all spoken for.

In all, we had commitments and deposits from the six families who wanted puppies, plus my brothers and cousin (who got a large discount but still agreed they should pay a little). What a fun day! We really enjoyed all of their visits and invited all the families to come back and visit any Saturday before we let their puppies go home.

And every single family came back every single Saturday or Sunday to play with their puppies! This included my family members and our friends who had selected Kane. It was amazing. We all got to be great friends.

We had decided that eight weeks was the right amount of time for us to keep the puppies with their mother, allowing them plenty of time to learn to socialize with their siblings. That's quite important if a dog is going to get along with other dogs in the future. By the time the eight-week mark was approaching, we wished we'd said ten weeks or twelve or never...because we were in love with everyone.

During the week after that first showing, Tunes and I seriously questioned whether we had kept the right two puppies. Especially the right girl. That one really smart female puppy really began to shine, becoming the "star" of the entire litter, and she was not the one we chose. A very nice couple from Santa Barbara chose her. They told us her name would be Sadie.

Tunes and I talked about modifying the toenail polish so that we could keep Sadie. We could have easily done it; neither her new parents nor anyone else would have ever known the difference. But in the long run, we decided to keep our word and good karma and did not switch any puppies.

The girl we kept, Yosemite, turned out to be the sweetest, smartest, most intuitive and delightful dog we ever had. Karma is for real.

Tunes put cute, little miniature scarves on each puppy. They were just adorable. As our family and new friends came by one-by-one to take their puppies, Tunes cried every time. I was close, too, several times. We just hated to be separated from any one of the wonderful group. It was truly bittersweet...and the end of an amazing adventure that we wished would last and last.

Each visit by a family to take home their new puppy was magical, too, because the people were so happy and appreciative. They told us we were the best dog breeders ever. While it was sad to see our babies leave, we were gratified to know that each one of Gracie's puppies would brighten the lives of many lovely people.

And luckily, it was not the last time we would all be together.

Chapter Twelve: The Party

A dog is the only thing on earth

that loves you more than he loves himself

- Josh Billings

Gracie, Yosemite, George II...and all the puppies, 2000

We encouraged the puppies' new families to stay in touch and send us photos and progress reports as the little guys grew up. Pretty much all of them did this, and we were getting cute photos and updates every week. Several families visited, too. They would always bring their puppy, plus puppy treats and sometimes wine or hors d'oeuvres for us humans.

It was really nice to maintain communication with many of the nice people who adopted puppies, and it was wonderful to see our former puppies as they grew up and got even feistier. We all considered ourselves to be friends after several weekends together and the common bond of the twelve adorable babies we were all raising.

It was definitely a thrill to hear stories and see photos of the individual puppies as they progressed in their new lives. Not so very long ago, they'd been tiny, helpless newborns, but now they were starting to come into their own.

Tunes had the inspired idea to hold a one-year-old birthday party for the puppies, and I was 100 percent on board with the sentiment. When she mentioned it to the various families, they were very enthusiastic.

A few months after the pups were born, we moved to a lovely house in Ventura – in the southwest corner of the Ojai Valley, about eight miles inland from the coast. The terrain was very much like the charming city of Ojai, with mountains rising up in the background, lots of big, stately oak trees and a closer proximity to nature than one gets within the confines of a city. It was roughly 30 miles from Santa Barbara and closer to Los Angeles, whereas the Solvang house was 30 miles to the north.

The new house was on five acres, on a hill above a lovely stream, with over fifty impressive oak trees, many around 100 years old, and a big old pool. The house was built in 1950 and was a fine example of Mid-Century Modern architecture. We painted it a light tan color with white trim. It was a great spot for Gracie to thrive and for her children, George Burns II and Yosemite, to grow up. They all loved to swim, we took exhilarating scooter runs every day, and they had plenty of room to roam around and experience "the country life." (And, I would be remiss not to add, to get real dirty.)

Most important of all, it was a serene spot where Tunes and I could continue to try to mend from the pain and trauma we'd been through.

We had the feeling that attendance would be very good at the puppy birthday party, and Tunes started planning months in advance. Her parties (I really can't take the credit) are legendary for their planning and attention to detail. These families did not know this, but they were going to be in for a treat. Meanwhile, the puppies' families made plenty of preparations themselves.

We sent out the invitations some two months in advance and were amazed to see that every family said they were coming. Some asked if they could bring other family dogs, and we said, sure, do it.

Some people called a few times to get advice on what to bring, throw out ideas and express excitement. Tunes loved strategizing with these new friends about decorating and planning food and treats.

A few of our regular friends who found out what we were planning wanted to come and experience this party with us. These were friends who had visited numerous times while the puppies were infants, and they had experienced Terryle's attention to detail in throwing theme parties. We welcomed them all.

There was a popular pet bakery in Santa Barbara named Three Dog Bakery, so we made it a point to visit one day to see what they offered. We were delighted to see a great variety of cakes and cookies offering dog and cat themes prepared with special, pet-healthy ingredients.

The bakery was very cheerful, with fun photos on the wall of pets and parties, ornate decorations, and close-ups of colorful cookies, pies and cakes. The outside sign was very welcoming, with a large, cute dog bone-shaped logo and Three Dog Bakery etched in a cute typeface. The retail workers greeted everyone with a smile and a welcome, and plenty of customers were there with their dogs on a leash. One lady was holding a cat festooned with colorful ribbons. Best of all was a huge glass showcase fronting the workers and just packed with yummy baked pet treats. (I say "yummy," but tempting as they looked, I did not try a sample.)

We ordered a large birthday cake shaped like a dog bone. We told the owner that we were having a one-year-old birthday celebration for a group of Golden Retriever puppies, and she asked if it was the one in Ventura. When Tunes said yes it was, the owner said everyone was talking about it and many people had been in to shop.

We bought a load of hot dogs for the guests of honor and picked up fried chicken plus accouterments for their human chaperones. Tunes made individualized, oversized stamps with a dog bone surrounding each puppy's name and then stamped them in gold on see-through plastic plates. It took hours to do it. She also had a puppy-themed tablecloth for our picnic table, plus theme napkins, cups and cocktail napkins. I made funny, dog-themed labels for several bottles of wine, and we put them on the bottles.

We decorated our outdoor picnic table in a total puppy theme, hung all kinds of banners, sashes and other decorations from the trees and made sure the key segments of the party would be in the shade of oaks since it was August and could be pretty warm.

Tunes' coup de grace was a big sign we hung between two trees. The sign was made of thirteen large, individual dog bone-shaped pieces of cardboard strung together by a ribbon. On the front side of each was a letter H-A-P-P-Y-B-I-R-T-H-D-A-Y, all done ornately in different colors. On the back side of each was a photo of each individual puppy at around three weeks old. The center card was a photo of all the puppies together and the caption: "Guess Which One is Yours?"

She also bought little notepads for each family (stamped with a cartoon Golden Retriever) and announced that the object of the game was for them to pick which puppy was theirs. Everyone loved the game, gushed at all the photos, and spent quite a while trying to pick out their own puppy. They were confident going in but pretty baffled trying to find their own when they looked at all the photos of the dogs on the back sides of the dog bones. It was hilarious hearing the families arguing about which puppy was theirs. As it turned out, only four families chose correctly.

One family from Solvang called a couple of days in advance to sadly decline the invitation. They had a family funeral they needed to attend. But all the rest showed up. With the puppies' father and grandfather, plus a few family dogs not from our litter, we had seventeen dogs total.

The families brought all sorts of treats and presents, too. We had a table full of dog-themed cookies, cupcakes, brownies, candies and two other festive cakes. All were designed to be tasty and healthy for dogs and looked amazing. There was a big pile of wrapped presents, as well.

Golden Retrievers at one year-old are nearly full grown lengthwise but still not at full weight. Their faces still have a hint of that puppy innocence and special "glow" but have progressed to 90 percent of what their adult faces will look like. Whereas they are mostly white-blonde at birth, they've taken on their final red-gold hue by one year.

And they totally act like puppies, if you're curious.

We wondered if the dogs would demonstrate any signs of recognizing special bonds with their reunited siblings, but they really didn't seem to. Of course, they were happy to see any other dogs and barked and ran around in an absolute frenzy of excitement at being inside this large gathering.

They also did not seem to show any special deference to their mother, so we never could tell if the puppies recognized Gracie. Likewise, she didn't act especially thrilled to be reunited with her offspring. In fact, Gracie and our two puppies were the shyest and least social at the beginning of the party since their home territory was suddenly being invaded by a gigantic horde of new dogs. Gracie stayed on the fringe, and George and Yosemite hid under the table. Luckily, they snapped out of it soon enough and joined the fun. How could they resist such an opportunity?

I would say, objectively, that the party was chaos. Really fun but borderline out of control, despite the meticulous planning. We tried to keep things flowing, and the humans certainly went with the flow, but the dogs were going berserk – running around the property, overwhelmed with excitement, running, playing, jostling and barking with all their "new" buddies.

When we served their hot dog lunches, they came back to the central picnic table, gobbled them up in no time flat and left immediately to resume their frenzied playing. They paid very little attention to the fact that there was a plastic plate designated for each puppy with the puppy's name stamped on it. We brought them back for assorted dog-healthy desserts, and they chowed all those courses down fast, too, leaving crumbs and icing everywhere. As the humans feasted on the fried chicken, plenty of puppies raced over and wondered why they didn't get that, too.

A couple of pups had ventured into the pool, but one of the high points of the day was when we all headed over to the pool and called the dogs. I wondered how many would go in for a swim, but it did not take long to find out. Wow – talk about a scene! About a dozen tried to get into the pool all at once; they were pushing and shoving, bumping and bonking down the pool steps or just plopping in from the sides. At one point, we counted fifteen dogs in the pool at once, swimming around, mostly clustering in the shallow end where they could stand up or jump on a buddy, splashing like crazy, jostling, excited as ever.

They acted crazy like they'd never gone swimming with fourteen other dogs before. Needless to say, most of our human guests who brought suits and had thoughts of swimming changed their minds. But a couple of intrepid children did go for it.

The pool was clouding with mud, however, and just to exacerbate that situation, many of the super-excited dogs would run out of the pool, run crazily around the yard a bit, roll in the dirt or find another way to get muddy, then race back into the pool. You've never seen a pool so black with mud.

After the guests left, our family members stuck around to laugh and talk about the day. It was one for the record books, and nobody had ever seen anything quite like it.

The next day, as I tidied up the yard, our pool maintenance man made his weekly visit. When he took a look at the astoundingly filthy pool, he got so very angry that it was a little frightening. He stormed around the pool, cursing. This guy was bulked up to almost inhuman size from working with weights and the likely use of plenty of steroids. The veins in his heavily muscled neck bulged dangerously.

"What the hell did you do?" he yell-asked incredulously. "You expect me to get this clean?"

"Just do your best," I suggested, quite humbly. "If it takes another visit or two, I understand."

He yelled at me a few more times, grumbled under his breath a lot and then walked up to me and went chest to chest, screaming at me for ruining the pool and expecting him to get it clean. I just nodded with sympathy. (I sure was not going to fight this behemoth.)

Long story short, he was in such a rotten mood on two subsequent visits that we had to get a new pool guy.

Year after year, on Tyler's (and our puppies') birthday, Tunes unpacked the 13 dog bones that comprised our sign and spread them across our front windows. From the front of the house, the letters spelled out "Happy Birthday." From inside, we could see every single puppy.

Tunes' puppy party was a big hit with everyone, and we got numerous thank-you notes in the subsequent week or two. People enclosed their best photos, which were hilarious and a treat to view. It was a great way to celebrate the special bond we all had for each other, and many of the puppy families stayed in touch for years. Mostly, though, it was so good to see each and every puppy one more time.

But I will say this: seeing all those Goldie puppies racing and romping around together was an emphatic affirmation that we had made the right decision, only keeping three.

Petey poses next to the pool a week before the invasion of his brothers and sisters

So does Tinker

One of the individual signs in Tune's hanging tribute to all the puppies at their first birthday party

Petey and Tinker after a nice, refreshing swim

Chapter Thirteen: Life Goes On

No one is going to appreciate your dog

the way you do.

- David Wilk

Here we are now in 2024. Petey and Tinker are eleven years old and still bright lights in our lives. We decided to move closer to the beach for a while, so now, instead of loads of space, forested hills and a pool to swim in, we walk Petey and Tinker to the beach every day where they can run around, explore, schmooze, with any and all other visitors, play ball and swim in the ocean.

I am continuing my new career of writing biographies (or ghost-writing autobiographies) for interested families. It all started some ten years earlier when a lady commissioned me to write a book about her parents. It was so much fun that I continued advertising for new clients. So far, I've written eighteen of these books and it is so interesting learning all about a person I had previously never met.

Tinker has slowed down quite a bit. She has health problems and sleeps a whole lot, but she still jumps up eagerly to go for her morning and afternoon walks – and without fail, she takes advantage of the chance to indulge in her number one lifelong priority – greeting people. If there's anyone in sight, Tink is determined to run up and say hello. Her friendliness has made her very popular in our new neighborhood. Everybody knows Tinker and seems delighted when she runs up, tail wagging furiously, her face mostly white but still very cute.

She likes other dogs, too, but people are her number one favorites by far, and when she runs up to someone with a dog, she always greets the person first. Tinker's absolute love for people is one of the foremost traits of Golden Retrievers, which is a key reason they are so popular.

Food is Tinker's other major priority, and we have to be careful because she will eat anything, anywhere, any time. Bite into a cookie or a piece of toast, and voila, she is there. Open a jar of peanuts or a bag of potato chips, and she could smell it from anywhere in the house. Place a sandwich on the coffee table for just a moment when you leave the room, and you may very well never see it again. It's like Tinker imposes a tax on anything edible. You are not allowed to eat something without her demanding her portion.

Every chance she gets, Tinker will position herself directly in front of Tunes or me, wagging her tail and lifting her head so warmly in the hope of being petted. In the evening, she'll cuddle up against our legs, pressing ever tighter, content to feel we are there with her. When we go to bed, Tinker will sleep with her bed touching ours, as close to us as she can get. She is as sweet as they come.

Petey is not exactly sweet, but he is a marvel. He is the most athletic dog we've ever had, and he's still going strong. People see him and are astounded that he's eleven years old. He wants to run everywhere, which clashes with the fact that Tunes and I have rediscovered the joy in just walking and enjoying the scenery.

Now that we live in a populated area, Petey usually has to be on a leash to prevent him from taking off to check out whatever captures his fancy.

This does restrain his roaming instincts but simultaneously yanks my arm right out of its ever-loving socket.

Petey pulls like a freight train. He could easily pull a car out of a ditch or handle sled duties in the Iditarod. On a trip to the beach, I don't theoretically have to take a step. I can just lift back onto my heels, and Petey will have me at the beach in 45 seconds. If I dared, I would put on some skates or ride a skateboard. I do not even come close to daring, however. If there ever was a dog who you do NOT want pulling you on a skateboard or tethered to the handlebars of a motor scooter, it's Petey. Luckily, I have not tempted fate. Also, I don't have either a skateboard or a motor scooter anymore.

When we get ready to go to the beach in the early evening, Petey runs back and forth through the house at near-top speed, overcome by his excitement. Tunes and I call this run "the wild thing." If we're running late, he makes it clear that someone is lagging in their responsibilities. He pauses in the wild thing dance long enough to give me an incredulous look.

There is no doubt about Petey's top priority in life. It is chasing the ball. That's why he likes the beach so much; we use a ball flinger to rocket the ball up and down the beach for him to chase, and he never wants to stop. Pete would rather chase the ball than eat, greet or be sweet. He likes people and can be a bit dicey with other dogs, but if the ball is in the air, rain or shine, he'll ignore everything to give chase.

He's good at ball fetching, too. I would have loved to see a ball-chasing contest between Petey and Gracie in her prime. Petey is faster and more aggressive, but he's not the ball-chasing savant that Gracie was. She paid attention to where the ball went and ran there with unerring accuracy. If she couldn't see it, she would sniff it out with one of the greatest noses in canine history.

Pete is all over the place, but he absolutely wants that ball. In fact, he's one of those dogs you might find with a ball in his mouth pretty much 24/7, just in case you possibly want to grab it and throw it.

Petey somehow conned me into taking a ball with me on our daily walk down and back up the hill at our old house. I'd throw it a few times, and wherever it went, he'd get it. I liked to use gravity to boost the distance and make him run farther. No problem, he would chase it downhill, then come running back up proudly to do it again.

On occasion the ball might bounce crazily off the driveway, out of control, down the hillside. That would not be a problem for Petey. He'd just plunge right down the slope, out of sight, to get it. It seemed cause for worry, but he always made it back. The bushes would rustle, branches would crunch, his steps would echo up loudly, and the dust would fly, but it was guaranteed that soon there would be Pete climbing back up into view with the ball clenched safely in his teeth.

There was a small meadow at our old house that sloped initially, then ran level for around thirty yards until it ended at a cliff that dropped off to the road and creek below. We went past it every day on our morning walk. I would bounce the ball down the hilly part, and Petey would run and chase it at astounding speed, snagging the ball with plenty of room to spare. But one day, I bounced it a little too aggressively, and while he got there in plenty of time, he proceeded to kick it just perfectly so that it traveled way further.

Sure enough, that ball bounced energetically toward the cliff. Sure enough, Petey raced right after it at full speed.

I started running top speed behind him, yelling, "Petey, no! Petey, stop! Nooo...!" but he had no interest at all in what I was saying. He was focused on the ball, and it was not getting away. The ball disappeared over the cliff, and to my horror, Petey followed right after it, leaping into the void and disappearing from view. I was running as fast as I could toward the edge of the cliff, feeling ever-increasing anxiety.

Pete was seemingly indestructible and had amazed me many times before with his feats. He'd leaped over picnic benches and yard sculptures multiple times and several times chased a ball at full speed straight into a tree, only to veer off at the very last millisecond – catching the ball before he changed directions. He'd run through thick bushes, barely losing a stride, or race through our cacti patch, amazingly dodging spines all the way. I'd been worried before, but the guy just defied injury so many times. He seemed so reckless that I had to wonder: doesn't some disaster have to happen sooner or later?

This time, he went right off that cliff and surely must have broken a leg...or his neck. "Petey," I screamed to myself, "why do you have to be so reckless?"

As I got to the edge of the cliff and looked down, I was stunned by what I saw. There was Petey, twenty feet down on a fairly narrow plateau, half-sunken into a thick bush, covered in brush, ball in mouth, looking up at me. That he landed on that plateau was one thing – absolute, supreme luck, I'd have to say. He couldn't have planned that when he sailed off the cliff. But how did he manage to have the ball?

I looked down in relief and astonishment while he calmly made his way around the side of the hill and soon joined me at the top, tail wagging with pride, ready to have another go. It was all pretty heart-stopping, but if you recall some of Petey's earlier episodes in this book, this barely makes the top three.

Tunes and I often talk about our wonderful canine friends who have departed. In our time together, we've shared our lives with Jenny, George Burns, Gracie Allen, Yosemite and George Burns II. And now, Petey and Tinker. What wonderful, exceptional companions they have been. These dogs spanned our entire married life and were significant and colorful parts of our lives every single day. They were all different, but they were each deeply cherished.

Dogs are so loving, loyal, instinctive, unique and colorful in their own astounding ways. Their purity and innate calm shine through the darkest times. Their trust is inspirational. Their loving gaze helps to calm even the most turbulent mood.

When we needed a smile, our dogs induced it without even trying. If we had to have a hug, they were all happy to oblige.

A dog is a man's best friend because she gives so much and asks so little. All she wants is to be fed, loved and to be with you as much as you can possibly manage. That is their reward. Your reward is so much greater.

The End

Tinker (foreground) and Petey enjoy sunset at the beach. Look closely and you'll see they both have their tennis balls

Petey emerges from the water

Petey romps in the meadow. The backside is where
he chased the ball off a cliff

Petey wants to know what adventure is coming up next

Tinker makes herself comfortable

Epilogue

While I was working on Amazing Dog Stories, several people volunteered interesting stories about their own dogs. I don't think there is any doubt that anyone with a dog has a great story or two – whether it's exciting, scary, heartwarming, happy or sad. So here's my idea:

I will create a blog that offers amazing dog stories sent in by you folks out there and credit each author. I'll post the blog on my website for this book, **AmazingDogStories.net**. When I accumulate enough good stories, I'll write another book – something like Amazing Dog Stories Part II – and anyone who submitted a story I use in the book will get a credit and a modest remuneration.

So email the website your best dog story, and if I like it, I'll edit it a bit, share it with the public and maybe put it in the next book.

You can also send your amazing dog story to:

Amazing Dog Stories/David Wilk

P.O. Box 1413 350 A. Street

Oxnard, CA 93030